Vicious Circle

A Salt Mine Novel

Joseph Browning   Suzi Yee

Published by Expeditious Retreat Press
Cover by J Caleb Design
Edited by Elizabeth VanZwoll

For information regarding Joseph Browning and Suzi Yee's novels and to subscribe to their mailing list, see their website at https://www.joseph-browning.com

To follow them on Twitter: https://twitter.com/Joseph_Browning

To follow Joseph on Facebook: https://www.facebook.com/joseph.browning.52

To follow Suzi on Facebook: https://www.facebook.com/SuziYeeAuthor/

To follow them on MeWe: https://mewe.com/i/josephbrowning

By Joseph Browning and Suzi Yee

The Salt Mine Novels

Money Hungry
Feeding Frenzy
Ground Rules
Mirror Mirror
Bottom Line
Whip Smart
Rest Assured
Hen Pecked
Brain Drain
Bone Dry
Vicious Circle
High Horse
Fair Game
Double Dutch
Dark Matter
Silent Night
Better Half
Soul Mates
Swan Song
Deep Sleep

Chapter One

Los Angeles, California, USA
2nd of March, 5:35 p.m. (GMT-8)

"I'm sorry, Vincent, I never meant for it to end this way," Megan Anderson said to her reflection in the bathroom mirror. She had repeated the words so many times that they risked losing their meaning, but she had to get them just right.

She broke eye contact and shook it out, resetting herself for another attempt. It wasn't bad, but she knew she could do better. She wanted to project the right feeling, but emotions were never really her strong suit, as the string of angry ex-boyfriends and one teary ex-girlfriend could attest.

She took a deep breath, lowered her shoulders, and raised her gaze from the floor. Her flowing honey blonde hair blew gently in the cross breeze from the open windows of her rented second-story room and her silvery eyes widened and sparkled. "I'm sorry, Vincent, I never meant for it to end this way." It was perfect and she pressed on, "But we were happy for a while, weren't we?"

A self-satisfied smile spread across her wide face. *That* was how she wanted it! It was soft and conciliatory with a dash of wistful, which was okay because she was speaking about it as if it were already over. It had taken her years to figure out how to walk that fine line.

She grabbed the battered script off the lidded toilet seat and hastily made notes in the margins using her personal brand of shorthand—a series of squiggles and pictorials to jog her memory later. It was the tone and eyes that sold it. She had given some variation of this speech many times in her twenty-four years, but the stakes had never been this high. She had a big audition tomorrow.

Since coming to LA, she'd worked as an extra on a few projects, bagged a handful of commercials, and even had one small speaking role on a subscription service series. However, this audition was for a more extensive part on a *network* show, something that would be aired on primetime TV and get her name in the closing credits—and not just a descriptor like "Second Woman" but a real, honest-to-god character with a name. She had a good feeling about this one. It was a rush job; the actress who had been cast for the role had gotten in a car wreck and the studio was crunched for time to get a replacement. If she did it right, she would be on to bigger and better things.

She moved on to the next lines and took them for a spin. "Nothing lasts forever. Everything dies eventually, even love." She watched her face perform the new lines but her eye was drawn to the spots on the bottom of the mirror. No matter how diligent she was, they always reappeared after brushing her teeth. She wet a corner of a hand towel and wiped them away, taking out her personal frustration on those little white dots.

These lines were more difficult for her. She understood them in a literal sense, but there was some deeper meaning that other people got and she didn't. She couldn't shake the feeling that they could be devastatingly impactful, if only she could tap into that zeitgeist. But no matter how hard she tried, she just couldn't *grok* them—a word she'd held fast to ever since she'd read *Stranger in a Strange Land* as a teenager. It perfectly encapsulated so much of her life's experience. Megan felt like she didn't *grok* many things that came easily to others.

It was hardest for her when she was a kid, and one of the best pieces of advice she'd ever gotten wasn't from her parents, teachers, or psychologists—it was from another kid, one of her super-smart friends in elementary school, who was now the youngest Michigan State Representative in history. He too had often felt the same way, and he approached it analytically instead of emotionally. That, coupled with the internet made assimilation a lot easier, even if she felt like she was constantly translating a foreign language.

She came to regard people like dogs, observing their behavior and body language and not relying solely on words. Just like how a dog's downward front and up rear meant "Time to play!" or how a side-eye meant "Give me some space," humans did the same thing, although she knew better than to say that out loud. People *really* didn't like being compared to dogs, regardless of how true it was. She'd learned to self-censor her real thoughts after paying the price of speaking honestly. Once she'd cracked the code, she began to get along better with her peers, much to her parents' relief.

But that didn't really help in auditions. Translating emotion from words on a page was challenging for her, and there weren't any nonverbal cues to guide her. Back in Michigan, she could read lines with her friends and trust them to get her to the right place, but she was on her own here. It was one of the few things she missed about home. She may not have understood her friends and family at a guttural level, but she knew they loved her and had her back. That was a luxury she didn't have in LA.

She left the bathroom and tossed the script and herself onto her unmade bed. She threw a mini-fit, silently flailing her long limbs out of fatigue and ennui. Her landlady was home and she didn't want to disturb her. What she needed was to clear her mind and come back at it fresh. A quick run would do her good. Her eyes turned to the browns and greens of Kenneth Hahn State Recreational Area outside her window.

She got out of bed and started a cup of herbal tea on the little private machine she kept in her room so it would cool while she was out. She didn't like hot tea and if she made it downstairs in the kitchen, her well-meaning landlady would invariably notice that she'd let her tea get cold and put in the microwave to reheat it for her. Megan didn't want to risk all that social interaction just for a beverage.

Not that she wasn't grateful; her mother always said to count your blessings. She was paying a paltry rate to stay in the spare room of a college friend's aunt's house to see if she really could cut it as an actress. If she'd had to side-hustle her way into paying market rate for LA housing, there wouldn't be enough hours in the day for her to audition.

It took her a few minutes to pick out a cute outfit and braid her hair. The prospect of running the rough paths was already lifting her mood. Her staccato steps on the stairs alerted Mrs. Johnson to her descent. "Is that you, Megan?"

"Yeah, just going out for a run. Be back soon," she called out and rattled her keys in her hand to let Mrs. Johnson know she hadn't forgotten them. She knew she didn't have to account for her comings and goings, but courtesy was one of the first behaviors she had recognized as being important, even if she didn't always understand its more complex expressions.

"Be careful and have fun," Mrs. Johnson replied.

Megan exited through the back door and locked the fence behind her. She cued up her running playlist before setting off along the dirt paths of the park. With every motion, she broadcast the unbridled exuberance of youth.

It wasn't much of a park, but it was big, elevated, and had great views of the city's lights during the evening. It was also one of the few places in the city where she could surround herself with trees, even if they were small copses of drought-resistant cork oak and desert willows. What her feet really longed for was to run barefoot on the rich cool soil of a Michigan summer, softly lit under a broad canopy, with bushes covered with wild berries for the picking.

Her urges struck her as ironic since she'd spent most of her youth plotting to leave Michigan. She'd assumed all the time she'd spent in the woods there was to escape the doldrums and constraints of Midwestern life, but even in LA, she found herself running to the natural spaces for comfort.

When she'd first arrived in LA, she was abuzz with energy, feeding on it like a bulb on an electrical wire. But after a few months, she'd felt drained, like a battery that needed recharging. She'd underestimated how much she relied on the woods to maintain her homeostasis. The proximity of Mrs. Johnson's house to the three-hundred-acre wild area smack dab in the middle of the LA sprawl was another reason she wanted to stay on her landlady's good side.

Her feet fell into rhythm with the music and she pounded up and down the hills at a quick pace. She soaked in the warmth and beautiful pinks, oranges, and purples of the setting sun. She filled her lungs with the smell of green, and softly—behind the music—she felt the sound of insects too impatient to wait for night to break. The distance and the destination meant nothing so long as she was hidden away among the trees, and the mix of mild euphoria became indistinguishable from the familiar burn in her legs.

By the time the shadows of the branches lost their distinct outline and coalesced into amorphous blobs, her concerns about the upcoming audition were gone. She was free—a maiden of the meadows, a child of the woods. Her mind was blank again, a clean slate.

As she focused on the dim path in front of her, she failed to notice the shadow that crept out from behind the concrete and wood pavilion placed along the trail, and how, once it had sight of her lost in her music and in her commune with nature, it raced toward her with frightening speed.

Chapter Two

Sumpter Township, Michigan, USA
2nd of March, 5:10 p.m. (GMT-5)

David Emrys Wilson sized up his opponent, his stance narrow and elbows close. *Think, think, think…* He drew his will around his hands before pressing forward in a series of decisive punches, chops, and jabs. The slim woman opposite him deftly swatted them away, simultaneously grabbing his attacking arm with one hand and punching him with the other. He pulled up his defenses to shield himself from the blows, but they kept coming with increasing speed and force. The last one knocked him down onto the neatly trimmed but still-dead Michigan grass. He was, in the parlance of the kids at the gym, getting his ass handed to him.

"You're as graceful as a hippo," Joan Liu—codename Aurora—said bluntly.

"Hippos are quite graceful in water, you know," he rebutted as he rolled to his feet. "I'm just out of my element." He went straight into a side attack and was again easily displaced and thrown.

"You're right. My apologies to all hippos for such an

unflattering comparison," she agreed as he flew by. This time, Wilson landed with an audible thud even with his augmentation and good form on the roll.

When Wilson had asked her to train him in augmentation magic a few months ago, Liu was surprised. Any practitioner could be taught to bolster their physical form with magical padding, akin to a boxer taping and gloving up before a fight. However, to magically augment beyond human speed, power, and protection required a predilection—an intrinsic ability that could be honed but not taught from scratch.

His tale of what had happened to him in the moors last December certainly sounded like high-level augmentation magic, and the fact that it was a defensive posture was consistent with a new augmenter—heaven only knows how many spills she'd taken before the age of ten that should have killed her but didn't.

The problem was the timing. Augmenters bloomed early. To this day, Liu's mother adamantly attributed her bad back and premature graying hair to her restless and wild child. Liu pegged Wilson somewhere in his early-to-mid forties, and he had been practicing the arts for at least a decade. He was well past the age of discovery and by all rights, should not have been able to do what he did.

Yet here she was, teaching him how to progress in the art of augmentation, the magical discipline in which a master could deal lethal attacks with just the tips of their fingers or remain uninjured after receiving killing blows. Wilson was just at the beginning of his training and would not be doing any of those moves anytime soon.

She'd started him on Wing Chun, the style of kung fu out of Southern China popularized by Hong Kong movies, except there were no wires here. It was good for fighting in constrained spaces because the stance was tight and maneuvers were simultaneously offensive and defensive. His nature was to rely on his Glock and its banishment bullets, so she thought that if he couldn't shoot an opponent and needed to rely on augmentation magic to survive the encounter, he was de facto in close quarters.

With his previous experience in boxing and Judo, he'd taken to it well. Early on in his training, he was able to summon the first rank of specialized augmentation powers, which was proof positive that he had an aptitude for it. However, he'd failed to progress any farther, and the past few weeks had been frustrating for both of them. Wilson was tired of getting the shit beaten out of him despite his best efforts, and Liu was tired of teaching against type.

Traditionally, augmenters had to work to *restrain* themselves, to limit the magic that seemed to flow so easily through them because of the karmic costs that came with it. The purpose of augmenter training was to attain instinctual control of their power—to use the least possible magic and no more. Ideally, modulating their power shouldn't require any more conscious thought than breathing.

When Liu had agreed to teach him, that's what she'd signed up for: teaching restraint. Given Wilson's natural predilection and the fact that his codename was Fulcrum, she'd figured it was going to be a cakewalk.

And frankly, so did he. He lived and breathed the idea of minimal force for maximal return. He was always looking for the exploitable widget at the crux of every problem or person. It was what made him a great CIA agent before he practiced the arts and became a master summoner—one of the few in the world—after he'd joined the Salt Mine.

He'd expected his fair share of setbacks and hurdles because that was part of learning any new skill. Liu was finding the summoning lessons he was giving her in exchange difficult, but she was still progressing. Unfortunately, he was not with her lessons and he didn't know why.

"It's time to wrap this up," she said, looking down at her watch. As Wilson rose, his breath steamed the air and his forehead was visibly sweaty, even in the chill of the early evening air. Liu remained unperturbed. Her breath wasn't labored and she was still bundled in her winter gear. "One more time. Focus, and give me all you got."

He nodded and centered himself, weaving all the frayed ends of his will together into one taunt rope. He launched into a final attack series, this time a little faster, pushing himself over the edge of suprahuman speed. She didn't throw him this time.

Instead, she counterattacked, leaving herself wide open for a counter-counterattack if he could just push himself into the next gear.

He blocked her attack and saw the opening, but couldn't muster the power to take it. As they sparred, she watched his face and saw him try and fail. As a little negative reinforcement, she opened up her speed and propelled him fifteen feet into the air. She wasn't worried about actually harming him because his augmented defense came easier than his attack, and perhaps a little bruised ego would help.

By the time he'd landed, she was waiting next to the cars, thirty yards away. "Not bad, but you can do better. See you at my place," she called out, unlocking her car door.

He raised a hand up to signal he was still alive and vocalized a single "K" from the ground. It had been a long session and while he was glad she was showing him the potential of what his augmentation could become, he was slightly worse for wear.

He groaned as he got up, but nothing was hurt, just his pride. He was mostly done panting by the time he got to his car. He unlocked his British racing green 911 and caught a glimpse of himself in the rearview mirror before things started steaming up. He kept his brown hair short and face shaven, and his brown eyes were always serious, even as he slowly allowed a little more whimsy in his life after his stint in Avalon.

He'd always been a small man, just under five-foot-five, but his time in the endless rolling green had stripped away much of his muscle mass to the point of being painfully thin. He'd regained some of the weight—this morning's scale read 134 lbs., which was twenty-six more than he'd had when Mau carried him out of Avalon—but he doubted he'd ever return to his old physique. He couldn't muster the desire to lift weights anymore, especially when augmentation training just wrecked him every time.

He turned the engine over and put the defroster on full blast; cracking the windows wasn't going to cut it this evening. He followed the rural roads back to the turn for I-94. They'd settled on augmentation practice at the farm the Salt Mine owned as it was an accessible location where Liu could do her wushu magic without causing a scene. It was rush-hour traffic, but thankfully it was in the other direction. He took the twenty-minute drive to his warehouse home, the 500, to make the mental switch from student to teacher.

While his sessions involved physical training, hers were largely spent doing research and hitting the books, starting with what she'd glossed over during the Mine's onboarding process. She'd come in knowing she was going to be a monster hunter and had focused on the information to that end: combat strengths and weaknesses, habits and habitats, tactics and groupings, etc. She'd skipped right over the philosophical and metaphysical details which were often at the heart of summoning rituals. She was an "all I need to know is how to kill it" type of practitioner, which reminded him of Hobgoblin, albeit sans the chaos factor that seemed to follow Buchholz wherever he went.

There had been a lot to cover, and not all of it academic. When he'd arrived at Liu's place for the first lesson, he'd discovered her summoning supplies consisted of an 18" x 18" piece of manufactured slate tile that she'd picked up at a home repair store and an old leather bag stuffed with a hodgepodge of arcane components in no particular order. The bottom of the bag was covered in that non-specific coating of dried, caked, and powdered dross of a handbag long overdue for a cleaning. Additionally, the only kind of summoning she'd done before was scrying, which was only technically summoning because the guides lived in another plane of existence—but because there was no compulsion to make them appear or speak to the summoner, it didn't really count in his mind.

After his initial assessment, Wilson went to the librarians for help. According to Chloe and Dot, Liu was par for the course. Historically, augmenters were, as a group, poor summoners. Their magic was about physically augmenting themselves beyond human limitations, while the magic used in summoning made the summoner vulnerable to the summoned. The two magics were diametrically opposed, and augmenters had a very difficult time overcoming their instinctual aversion to vulnerability. It was completely reasonable but ultimately a mismatch for performing summoning magic. More often than not, it resulted in a failed ritual.

Wilson had warned Liu up front. The inscription could

be perfectly written, the incantation spoken right, the correct accoutrements in place, but if the practitioner couldn't work the magic, nothing was going to show up in their circle. Undeterred, she pressed ahead with Wilson's help.

As she had done for him, he selected training that would be the most useful to her. She was never going to set up a dedicated ritual room or have a series of silver-poured pentagrams and circles set into the floor, but she could learn how to safely summon supernatural creatures to identify or track her prey. There was much that the guides could not see, and summoned creatures could be coerced.

Tonight was Liu's first solo summoning. She would be responsible for making the circle, writing the inscription, saying the incantation, and powering the ritual with her—and only her—will. Wilson would be on standby to observe and intervene, if necessary, but mostly he would be a silent observer to gauge her work.

After much consideration, he advised Liu to summon a winged hordeling. Hordelings were minor devils, the foot soldiers of hell's armies. Hell was constantly at war with itself and millions of hordelings died on a daily basis. The bulk reincarnated into even lesser types of devils; Hell did not reward failure. Hordelings that survived several combats or participated in great victories would be ritually executed for an upwards reincarnation, joining the ranks of the more powerful. That was the way it was in Hell, up and down the ladder of hierarchy, and always looking up at the next rung even though the top could never be seen. Winged hordelings were the least dangerous of the bunch and served as scouts. They were well informed without having any stature in hell's legions—the perfect field servant. Imps were better, but Ivory Tower's extensive use of them made Wilson wary of accessing their information.

When he got home, he took a quick shower and grabbed a fast bite. Before he left, he opened a can of tuna for Mau, not that she would starve without it. He suspected that she was getting extra tuna on the side from Martinez given the distinctly oily shine he occasionally found on her black furry face. It was a good thing mummified cats didn't have to worry about mercury poisoning.

Liu lived in a two-bedroom condo on the third floor in a complex near Woodmere Cemetery, a little more than a mile away from Zug Island and the Mine. The second bedroom was mostly empty, and Wilson had convinced her to turn it into an impromptu summoning room after a bit of negotiation—she wasn't interested in anything permanent.

He rang her doorbell and the woeful paucity of runes on the frame ate away at him while he waited. Most were anti-surveillance, which made sense—if someone can't see or find you, they couldn't target you. Still, it ran against his grain. The 500 was a veritable fortress, both physically and magically. The only reason Mau could come and go as she pleased was because there was nowhere the feline legend couldn't go. Even the Mine couldn't keep her out and had to settle on knowing when she entered and left and where she'd roamed.

Liu answered the door with a harried look on her face. "Come on in, I'm almost done," she informed him and immediately spotted the extra bag he was carrying. "What's that?" she asked after he closed the door behind him.

"Something for you," he said tersely as he reflexively scanned his surroundings. The interior had that recently-tidied-for-guests look that he'd come to expect, and the stack of pizza boxes on the refrigerator was a little taller than last time. "I thought it would come in handy, something like a summoners travel kit so you can keep track of what you have and when you are getting low."

Liu opened the leather bag and saw all the little pockets and compartments neatly filled. It was a mini version of his own repurposed leather medical bag, sans the accoutrements for the more advanced summonings. She was speechless. Every time she thought Wilson was a complete dunce, he pulled something like this. She almost felt bad for tossing him around so much this afternoon. "Thank you. That was very considerate."

They entered her second bedroom, which had become a storage room over the years. All the things she no longer used but hadn't gotten rid of ended up there. She'd shifted things around to accommodate the square yard slab of black granite Wilson insisted she buy, and it rested underneath the bland

90's light fixture that came with the place when she bought it.

Wilson took a seat on the daybed against the wall while Liu knelt on the carpet next to the stone and continued working from memory. Most summoners would have used a book or other reference to draw a summoning circle and inscription, but since he was gearing her training to summon small fiends and faeries that one would commonly want to employ in the field, doing it from memory became part of the test.

The chalk squeaked against the stone as Liu finished the last ascender, making sure it touched the circle. She set the chalk into the plastic container of her new summoning bag and pulled out the rest of the components she would need from their cubbyholes. She was more a shoes than handbag sort of woman, but she had to admit, the accessory helped.

"Ready?" he asked once she had everything out.

She nodded. He switched off the light and backed out of the room to observe from the hallway. First, she lit the five tallow candles that stood on the points of the pentagram—beeswax wouldn't cut it because hordelings liked the smell of burning flesh. She applied a series of unguents and pastes to her face and arms as the candles lightly smoked. Properly anointed, she lit a small piece of incense charcoal in the brass burner and began the invocation proper. Much to his delight, her Latin was perfect, rid of the accent that she'd had when she'd first started training.

After the final syllable was uttered, Liu pulled out one of

her many daggers and pricked her left thumb, drawing a bead of blood. She dropped it in the center of the now-hot charcoal. It sputtered and smoked, giving the aroma of burning tallow a sweet, sticky, ferrous note. He could feel her draw in her will and spin it around the circle, completing the ritual.

A puff of sulfurous smoke filled the circle and then cleared, leaving behind a small winged figure. It was naked and hairless, its red skin smooth as a leather sofa. Its bat-like wings extended from a prominent hunch on its bent back. It held a small trident in one hand while the other hand dangled by its side, nearly touching the granite slab.

It was part of the reason he'd selected a winged hordeling for her first solo summoning—it was just the right size for the slab of granite. While a practitioner could technically summon a devil in any size circle, there was a better return on expended will if the devil's natural size was close to the size of the circle. If the creature was too big, it required more power to contain it in bounds, and if the circle was oversized, it would require more will than necessary upfront to power the summoning. He'd deliberately given her the Goldilocks zone of devil summoning.

"You have summoned me," it rasped between oversized canine teeth.

"I have," Liu responded firmly, but the strain of the summoning showed on her face. Wilson docked her a few points and made a mental note to remind her to remain as unanimated as possible when dealing with a summoned creature. The very act of summoning created a supernatural channel and it was important to deliberately deny them any information. The creature in her circle wasn't the guides; a hordeling wasn't fair or neutral. Even the lowest of devils were evil and wouldn't hesitate to rip a human to shreds if given the chance.

The devil was slow to respond and started pressing its will against hers. Even though the circle protected her from all but the tiniest bit of the winged hordeling's power, it would still try to charm her into breaking the circle. Wilson had warned her the weaker, less intelligent devils *always* tried that.

"Enough," Liu said flatly. Her tone pleased Wilson—it was a voice that demanded obedience and it struck fear into the little fiend. "I have mastered you to my will and require a service from you."

After spinning around the circle and testing all sides, the hordeling succumbed to the inevitable. Taking to wing, it flew so that its eyes were just below the level of its summoner's, a posture of deferential respect. "What is it that you ask of me?" it begged ingratiatingly, but its voice could never be called pleasant. It sounded like two pieces of wet leather rubbing against each other.

Its wings beat furiously to keep it aloft, creating small drafts that circulated the room. When the breeze reached the unlit light fixture in the center of the ceiling, it dislodged a large flake of dust that drifted down toward the circle

"The dust!" Wilson yelled and gathered his will.

Liu saw the string of dust just as it was about to land on the chalk. Without hesitation she drew one of her blades and dove *through* the protective circle. She knew the dagger wouldn't banish the creature like normal—it was impossible for a summoner to wield magic against the creature they had summoned during the ritual itself. However, there was nothing in the rules that said she couldn't use magic on herself. In one swift, singular slice—almost faster than Wilson could see—she'd struck so fast and hard that it decapitated the devil. The winged hordeling's head fell next to its body, both leaking a sable ichor over the edges of the black granite slab.

She immediately got up and grabbed the roll of paper towels she had nearby. "Shit. I hope I don't have to get the carpet cleaned," she grumbled as she passed Wilson on the way to the bathroom. Never one to waste an opportunity, he started filling empty vials and jars with bits of the winged hordeling. One never knew when such would be useful.

After a while, the water in the bathroom shut off. "I guess I failed," she said from the doorway, wiping down her now clean face and arms.

"Yes," he said emphatically. "Anytime the circle is broken for any reason, the summoning is a bust."

"But I did everything right and actually summoned it. That's gotta count for something," she objected as she sheathed the cleaned dagger.

Wilson checked the caps on the vials of devil ichor before tucking them into his bag. "True, but you're going to have to be a little more thorough in your cleaning. Accidents can't happen with summonings. That's a fast way to get dead."

"It's no big deal. I took care of it," she dismissed his caution as she blew out the candles and smothered the charcoal.

Wilson rubbed his temple and tried to explain it in terms she would understand. "This time it was, but if you hadn't noticed the dust before it broke the circle, things could have been different."

She shrugged as she pulled out a tarp for the body and saturated paper towels. "So I'll get a cleaner in here more often and stick to summoning things I can kill without a problem."

Her blasé attitude grated on his last nerve. "You know what you are? You're the kid that doesn't study because they are smart enough to skate by without doing any more than they must. You're a master augmenter. You can destroy pretty much anything you'd summon because you won't bother summoning anything faster, tougher, or more dangerous than yourself. So what if you fail? It's not like you're really threatened. Worse case for you is dealing with the body and getting a carpet cleaned afterward.

"But if you ever want to summon things that know more, you're going to have to sweat the small stuff. Summoning is all about the details—the part that you find so boring because you don't feel any danger in the process. You have to hone that discipline on the puny creatures if you want it to be instinct when you summon creatures you can't kill outright."

Liu had never seen Wilson so emotive before. About anything. She weighed his words as she wrapped the small body in the tarp. "Point taken," she conceded. "But as long as we're giving notes, I have a theory about why you're not progressing as an augmenter." Wilson didn't like the hint of iron in her voice but kept his mouth shut. He had started it.

"During all that time I've been cooped up in the library busting my ass with all this summoning research, I found some historical writings about augmentation as well. According to Glitonea, who you'll recall is one of the nine witches of Ystawingun, the power of augmentation arises from mastery of strong emotions. Those who are more capable of feeling deeply are more capable of altering their body. I had hoped getting your ass kicked repeatedly was going to be enough, but it would appear not.

"If *you* ever want to cultivate your augmentation further, you're going to have to get in touch with your feelings instead of carefully reining in everything behind that impassive demeanor you've cultivated so well. It's stifling your progress, in more ways than one."

She trussed up the bundle with rope and tied it with surgeon's knots. This was not her first corpse. "Now if you'll excuse me, I have a body to dispose of and cleanse with fire."

Chapter Three

Detroit, Michigan, USA
3rd of March, 6:10 a.m. (GMT-5)

The rumble of the diesel trucks leaving the massive postal service distribution center across the street from the 500 pulled Wilson out of his sleep, but his shower last night provided a few extra minutes to roll around under the heavy comforter this morning. He'd slept hard but not soundly, uncertain what to do about his augmentation training. He was not prepared to get in touch with his feelings, but he wasn't ready to walk away from a new branch of the arcane arts, either.

He reluctantly pulled himself out of bed. There were calisthenics and stretches to be done, ablutions to perform, and a suit to don before he got his morning coffee, already programmed on his machine's timer. After the initial disruption caused by his prolonged stay in Avalon, he was approaching something closer to his normal habits.

When he entered the kitchen, Mau was waiting by her bowl: a custom silver affair with "KITTY" emblazoned on the side in real gold. Leader had advised it as a way of enticing the cat that could go anywhere to stay close at hand, and it had worked. Although Mau had said nothing when gifted it, she'd never since failed to breakfast with Wilson whenever he was at home, provided he had tuna, of course.

However, she still didn't call it tuna; it was "the fish from the metal circle." Wilson saw no reason to challenge her. It wasn't like she was talking to anyone else, so what did it matter what she called it? But on principle, he still called it tuna. From Mau's perspective, she called things what they should be called and if he didn't understand, it was *his* fault for not knowing the proper names of things. The great tuna debate pretty much encapsulated their association—Wilson hesitated to call it a relationship or even a cohabitation, and Mau knew what it was regardless of labels.

This morning, as she inhaled her tuna, she could smell the difference on him—Crawling Shadow was crawling more than normal. After she finished her breakfast, she postponed her postprandial grooming and leapt onto the table where he was drinking his foul liquid and reading the tragedies of the world the humans called news. She sat on her haunches and gave him audience.

"Mau?" Wilson tentatively said, looking up from his tablet.

Mau slightly tilted her head sideways to indicate he could speak.

He shut the lid on his tablet and folded his hands together. "I have a question for you, but you don't have to answer if you don't want to."

Mau didn't move or bat an eye—there was no need to respond to the obvious.

"How do feel about Hor-Nebwy?"

Nothing, Mau responded in Wilson's head. She could speak aloud, but as she was pretending to be a regular cat, she used head-speak with him whenever possible.

"What do you mean by nothing?" he asked for clarification. "Nothing as in 'I don't think about Hor-Nebwy,' or nothing as in 'whenever I think about him I think he's nothing'?"

Nothing, as in nothing, Mau thought at Wilson. *Let me show you*. The black cat's green eyes flashed and she thought about the ancient mummy magician that had brought her soul back from the land of the dead, put it into a living vessel only to ritually kill and mummify her thousands of years ago. She then *pushed* her feelings toward Crawling Shadow and blinked.

A wave of indifference suddenly crashed over Wilson, and he leaned back in his chair in shock. "You can project emotions?!"

You can't? No wonder your kind spends so much time babbling to each other.

Wilson wryly smiled. "So you have no feelings of resentment or anger toward the being who enslaved you to his will for millennia? Nothing about all those lost years?"

No.

Wilson waited for more of an answer, but after none came, he merely said, "That's remarkable."

Mau didn't respond as everything she did was remarkable.

To say more would have been redundant or boastful, and she was neither. But she knew that was not the end of the conversation. Crawling Shadow was writhing even more than before. Something important was happening.

"How do you do that? How did you stop caring?" he asked.

Mau lay down on the table like the Sphinx. He was asking all the wrong questions. Clearly, this was going to take a while. *I did not stop caring. I constantly care.*

Wilson was genuinely confused. "But you just said you don't care about Hor-Nebwy."

I don't, she reiterated.

"But you cared when you first arrived here. You were very adamant about not going back—that you were *free.*" He could still hear the urgency with which the cat had spoken that night when they revealed what had transpired in Avalon to Leader, LaSalle, and Chloe and Dot.

I care about what should be cared about. At that point, Hor-Nebwy was to be cared about. He is not now, she patiently spelled it out for him.

"So how did you stop caring about him?" Wilson pressed.

I did not stop caring about him; he stopped being something to care about, so the caring stopped.

Wilson felt like they were going around in semantic circles and tried rephrasing his query, "So how did he stop being something to be cared about?"

Her tail flicked off to the side; now, he was asking better

questions. *I am free. He does not know I am free. He poses no threat. He is tricked.*

"But he could figure out he was tricked at any moment," he pointed out.

That is unlikely, but if it happens I will then care as there would be something to care about. Caring about what hasn't happened is foolishness. It is almost as foolish as caring about a happening that has ended.

She waited for him to process that in silence; it took humans a long time to understand things, if they ever did. She could feel the pressure behind his next precisely phrased statement. "I've been told that I need to feel strong emotions if I'm to succeed in an endeavor."

Is the endeavor something that you want to succeed in? she asked socratically.

"Yes."

Than feel strong emotions, she stated plainly.

"But not feeling strong emotions is what has kept me alive. It's what keeps me safe. And keeps those around me safe. I have too much in my past to feel strongly about. When you dredge the bottom of the ocean, you find old bones."

You are not the ocean. There are no old bones, she said flatly.

"I'm being metaphorical, Mau."

I know what metaphor is. You are still not the ocean and you do not contain any bones.

Wilson couldn't resist himself. "Technically, I do contain

bones."

You are Crawling Shadow. Shadows contain no bones, she corrected him.

He dropped it because he knew Mau *wouldn't* and got back on track. "Tell me, how would *you* summon up strong emotions if your caring stops when something stops being something to care about?"

Needing to feel strong emotions is a happening. I would then care.

"But when the need was over, you would not care as the need has passed," he tried to suss out her logic.

Yes! Mau thought a little too loudly in her excitement that Crawling Shadow was finally talking sense. *When a happening is over, the caring for the happening ends.*

Wilson took a sip of his second espresso and mulled over Mau's point of view. "Would you mind if I petted you for a while?" he asked.

That is acceptable, the green-eyed cat replied, putting her head down on her paws. There was no space for her in his lap with all the agitation that whirled around him. He started to stroke her silky ebony coat with one hand and held his coffee with the other.

There is no past or future, Crawling Shadow. There is the eternal now until the now ends and then everything dies and is forgotten. Do not let this worry you; that is a foolish response to the happening. Wilson didn't respond but scratched behind her ears. She purred when he hit just the right spot.

Over the next five minutes, Mau felt Crawling Shadow settle. When he finally departed for work, she jumped onto the sill of one of the windows on the top story of the 500. In the distance, around Wilson's green car, the cat watched the shadows swirl—not yet stilled, but calmer. Satisfied, Mau licked one paw and washed her face, contemplating where she wanted to go to today.

Wilson drove on autopilot and passed the normal security measures with barely a second thought. His brief conversation with his cat resonated with him. Throughout the morning, Mau's words returned: *That is a foolish response to the happening.* Between filing paperwork in his Art Deco office, reading the daily intelligence reports, and even during a trip to the library to speak with Chloe and Dot, it echoed: *That is a foolish response to the happening.*

As he ate a quiet lunch in the canteen alone, he couldn't decide which was weirder: that his talking cat was some type of Zen Stoic or that he was seriously mulling over the validity of her words. *That is a foolish response to the happening.* It was an old philosophy but when Mau said it to him telepathically, it felt revolutionary.

Wilson was sitting in his leather and walnut swivel chair absentmindedly tapping his pen on his French polished walnut desk shortly after lunch when the olive box on the corner of his desk flashed and buzzed. He sat up and pressed the button.

"This is Wilson."

David LaSalle's precise tenor came through the speaker. "Leader wants to see you right away."

He noted the time on his Girard-Perregaux before answering. "I'm on my way. Fulcrum out."

Wilson spent the five minutes it took to get from his office to Leader's to clear his mind of all the navel gazing. Leader didn't summon an agent ASAP without just cause. When he exited the elevator to the fourth floor, he found her assistant at his desk, rapidly typing away.

At six-foot-three and two hundred thirty pounds, LaSalle was a bruiser. He was skilled in close combat and there were few weapons he wasn't at least familiar with, if not proficient. But he was far more than just muscle. His administrative acumen was bar none. Regardless how many things were thrown at him, he kept the Salt Mine running smoothly. No matter how strange the request, he'd never failed to get Wilson what he needed in the field. And he was no slouch in the magic department, either. Wilson didn't know the full scope of LaSalle's arcane abilities, but he knew enough to never underestimate him.

The two men made eye contact and exchanged a series of nods, which sufficed as pleasantries between them. LaSalle immediately stopped his work, secured the computer and documents, and ushered Wilson into Leader's office.

"Leader, Fulcrum is here," her towering secretary-slash-bodyguard informed her. She took her nose out of the file and from her vantage, the pair looked like an ill-conceived *Twins* reboot.

"Thank you, David. Fulcrum, take a seat," Leader addressed them both in one stroke. There was never any doubt who she was talking to. LaSalle was always David, and Wilson Fulcrum. The only time he remembered her calling him anything else was when he'd invited them into the 500 upon his return from Avalon.

The office was the same as always, down to the position of the oversized white leather chairs, but Leader stood out from the bank of filing cabinets behind her desk. She was wearing a dark gray suit with a pink buttoned-down shirt underneath, a far cry from her homemade sweaters and khakis. At barely five feet tall, everything had to be tailored to fit, and her power suit made her overwhelming presence and hawkish gaze more daunting than usual.

She dug another file out of one of the bottom cabinets and placed the black folder on her desk. Wilson's interest was immediately piqued—the Mine stopped using black files in 1962.

"We have a rare opportunity, Fulcrum," she said, sweeping the brief across the massive desk between them. "An unsolved case opened in 1956."

Wilson flipped through the old paper with care. "The Butterfly Killer…wasn't the last death in the late 1970s?" he asked in disbelief.

"1978," she confirmed. "This morning, we got an anonymous tip about a magical death in LA through the hotline. When the analysts checked it out, they verified that in the wee hours of the morning, LAPD found a badly decomposed corpse covered in butterflies in a local park."

"Parameters?" he asked as he handled the photos gingerly, their edges worn by time.

"I'm sending you in as FBI and the sixth floor is at your disposal on this one," she answered. "It's never made sense. I want you to make sense of it."

"Because now we have saltcasters," he surmised. Harold Weber had invented salt-casting technology in the 1970s, but the original device was huge, the same way the first computers took up entire rooms. The first man-portable wasn't until the 1980s, a large backpack that had to be attuned to the wearer each time in order to work. It wasn't until the late 1990s that Weber got it down to the ivory tube, and the vape pen was his latest coup in the never-ending process of making a saltcaster even smaller and easier to use in the field.

"Precisely. That may be enough to tip the scales in our favor this time," she concurred as she reached for the intercom button on her desk. "David, where are we on digitizing the Butterfly files?"

"I should have them in Fulcrum's inbox before he flies out," the steady tenor avowed. They could hear typing in the background.

"Excellent. Thank you, David," she said before releasing the button.

Leader turned her indomitable gaze to Wilson and her gray eyes darkened. "I don't like loose ends. Put this one to bed."

*****

LaSalle was true to his word: Wilson got the message with attachments on his phone while he was waiting for his boarding group in Detroit Metropolitan Airport. He didn't usually cut it this close, but once Wilson opened the files, he saw why.

All the files the Mine generated for their agents were character-searchable, which wasn't a problem for content created in the digital era. Older documents were scanned and put through Optical Character Recognition software. However, more than half the documents in the Butterfly Killer files were originally typed on photocopy-resistant light blue pages as an old security measure, which caused the current OCR program problems. It still produced text, but it was often so garbled that it took almost as long to unscramble as it did to simply retype the documents.

The work could have been passed off to one of the upper-level grunts if it had been less sensitive or if they had more time to break it up and delegate sections to different people, but Wilson had no doubt LaSalle did this himself. When Leader flagged something as important, it took priority.

The direct flight to LA was just under five hours, giving him plenty of time to read up on the Butterfly Killer. It was a case study in the bizarre and even more intriguing because it was never solved. Salt Mine agents didn't often do cold cases because there always seemed to be plenty of work in the here and now to keep them busy.

Once the plane reached altitude and the seatbelt light was switched off, Wilson pulled out his phone. The newly formed Salt Mine first discovered the Butterfly Killer in the summer of 1956 when a series of three people were found in dead in Hackensack, New Jersey over a period of three months. All three victims were found in a state of advanced decay and covered by butterflies of six different species, the majority of them monarchs. All three were male, twenty to twenty-nine years of age, and two had violent criminal records while one was apparently clean. The police couldn't find any connections between the men apart from their residence in the Garden State.

The second set of deaths was found when the Mine started digging after the New Jersey deaths. They'd occurred nearly thirty years earlier in Atlantic City. Three dead women were found in a hotel room covered in butterflies. The forensic records had been destroyed in a fire, but the newspapers indicated the victims were known criminals, two sisters and a close associate. Again, all three were in their twenties.

The third and final deaths took place in Pismo Beach,

California in 1978. This was different than the others. Only two men were found, seniors at California State; neither had criminal records. Technology had improved since the 1950s and the forensic investigation team had found large amounts of butterfly sex pheromones on the bodies. It accounted for the mass of butterflies on the corpses, but not what killed them and how they became so decomposed over a short period of them. The investigation looked into local lepidopterists but nothing had come of the search.

Wilson weighed the facts as they were. The victims were all in their twenties and their bodies were found in a similar state, but that was where the similarities ended. Some clusters were found together while others happened sequentially. Genders and backgrounds were mixed. They occurred in different locations, but all were relatively coastal.

Wilson had no information on the body found this morning, but if it was related, it was nearly a hundred years from the first incident in Atlantic City to the latest in LA. If the perpetrator was human, they were most certainly a copycat, but he'd learned long ago to never make such assumptions when it came to the supernatural.

Chapter Four

Los Angeles, California, USA
3rd of March, 5:15 p.m. (GMT-8)

"Is this guy ever going to show up?" Detective Jose Huertas grumbled, checking his watch as he spun a pen around his hand.

"I could have sent you to the airport to pick him up," Detective Kate Fawcett deadpanned. She looked up from her computer screen. "Perhaps you could get on some of that paperwork instead of practicing your manual dexterity."

"Paperwork doesn't impress the ladies," Huertas responded, turning slightly so that Fawcett could get a better look at what he liked to call his "mad skillz."

"Yeah, pen spinning drives all the women wild," she drolly replied as she restarted her typing.

"What can I say? I like the strange ones," he grinned before turning serious. He even put down his pen. "Ever met the guy before?" Fawcett had to give her junior officer credit. He was a yahoo, but he generally knew when to turn it off, which made him good comic relief when the stress of the job pressed down too hard.

"Once, a couple of years ago," she answered him. "Brooks did most of the talking then." Huertas did the math; it had to be more than four years ago, back when Brooks had held her position and she was in his shoes. "If I'm remembering properly, guy was a G-man straight out of an old movie. Nice suit, but not too nice. Professional and deferent, but you knew he wasn't asking, he was telling." She paused and added a single-word descriptor, "Focused."

Huertas nodded. He'd never worked with the FBI before. Then again, he had never seen such a messed-up crime scene, either. He prided himself on keeping it together on the job, but everything about it was unnerving. And he sure as hell never thought he would have to catch butterflies in the line of duty.

The phone on his desk rang, breaking his ruminations. He picked up the receiver and gave his smoothest "Detective Huertas." Fawcett smirked but said nothing. "Thanks, I'll be right down," he told the front desk clerk. Huertas put on his jacket and straightened his tie while he addressed his senior officer. "Speak of the devil…"

He strolled through his precinct with ease and collected Special Agent David Wilson of the FBI from the front. Wilson wasn't what he'd expected at all. He was small, thin, and entirely unimposing, although he was impeccably dressed, from his expensive leather briefcase to his bespoke suit. Even his shoes looked fancy. "Special Agent Wilson?" Huertas greeted him, holding out his hand.

Wilson nodded. "Detective Huertas, I presume?" He shook his hand and the firmness of the grip took the young detective by surprise. "Pleased to meet you."

"Detective Fawcett is upstairs. If you'll follow me?" he said as he held the door open for Wilson before taking the lead. Huertas tried to get a read on the stone-faced man as they rode the elevator to the sixth floor. "Come out to LA often?" he tried to make conversation.

"No," was the only response he got. Huertas took the hint and awkwardly waited for the floors to pass under them.

Detective Fawcett was waiting for them when the elevator arrived. Huertas made introductions and gladly passed the fed off to her. "I don't know if you remember, but we've worked together before," she said as she led them to the small conference room reserved for the meeting. Normally the investigation would be centered at their desks, but whenever they dealt with the feds, the investigation leapfrogged to the top of the heap and garnered privacy.

"I'm sorry, I don't remember," Wilson said bluntly, although that was a lie. Of course he remembered—clearing out a vampire nest in Rancho Palos Verdes was not something one easily forgot. But denial put more social pressure on her and any deterrent he could provide to prevent a stroll down memory lane was worth employing.

"It was about a series of exsanguinatory murders in Encino..." she persisted as they entered the conference room.

"Ah yes, now I remember," he feigned recollection. That was the problem with cops—they were like a dog with a bone. "If I recall, I dealt mostly with your partner on that one."

"Detective Brooks," she affirmed. "Only we never heard what happened and I've always been curious."

"It was drug related and handed over to the DEA. I'm afraid I'm just as in the dark as you are," he replied, reusing that old chestnut. Both detectives gave nonverbal gestures of commiseration. All law enforcement understood having their cases pulled from them due to jurisdiction. "Perhaps you can walk me through what we know about this unfortunate soul?" he redirected attention to the murder board along the wall.

It was pretty bare, but that was excusable considering they'd only found the body this morning. Fawcett started with the facts. "At 5:30 a.m., a jogger found a mound of butterflies along the trail during his typical morning run. As he approached, he saw a hand underneath all the fluttering and called 911. Uniforms secured the scene at 5:45. The body was in a severe state of decomposition and CSI was unable to lift prints. The remains are at the morgue awaiting autopsy. We're running the teeth against dental records but we still don't have a firm ID."

It's always a jogger, Wilson thought to himself as he looked over the pictures of the body, pre and post butterfly dispersal. He saw no overt signs of ritual casting in the dirt. "Do you have the personal information for the jogger?"

"On file, but we haven't followed up yet," Huertas fielded

the question.

Wilson nodded; it wasn't atypical at this stage. "How remote is the area?" He'd reviewed the satellite images, but that didn't tell him anything about the amount of traffic that passed through there.

"Not very. The park in general is a popular destination for locals, and the body was found on a designated running trail, albeit a dirt path and not one of the paved ones," Huertas answered.

Wilson looked at the map stuck on the board. "How accessible is the park?"

"There are lots of trails in and out from the parking lots and the neighborhoods to the east. Uniforms started canvassing the area this afternoon but haven't uncovered anything promising," he answered.

Wilson nodded—a body dump in that state of decay would be unlikely, and there would be pictures of tracks on the board if they had found any nearby. "Anything strike you as usual about the scene?"

Huertas and Fawcett exchanged quizzical looks. "Besides a heavily rotted corpse that smells like roses, found on a popular jogging trail where it couldn't have gone unnoticed for long enough to decompose, and covered in butterflies? No," he responded with a hefty dose of sarcasm.

Wilson raised an eyebrow. "It didn't smell?"

"Oh, it smelled, but more like a flower shop and less like

the morgue," the detective replied.

The gears in Wilson's head started turning. "When's the autopsy scheduled?"

"Tomorrow morning. Definitely before lunch," Fawcett responded.

"Is there a way I could be present?" Wilson requested.

Fawcett's head cocked back. "I'll see what I can do."

Huertas's curiosity got the better of him. "Can I ask what's the FBI's interest in all this?"

Wilson took a seat and opened his Korchmar Monroe attaché. He passed over the documents the Mine had prepared for his cover, mostly accurate but anything supernatural in nature had been redacted and altered. "I'm sure I don't need to tell you, but the information in the files is confidential: please don't share it with any of your fellow officers. I'll give you some time to become familiar with the material while I look over what you have so far."

Wilson took down the name and home address of the jogger in case he needed to interview him and held up the thin file as a prop while he observed the two detectives. There was a lot he could tell about two people based on how they shared a single file. Fawcett was no-nonsense and Huertas was comfortable in his supportive position—the sign of a good boss, a good subordinate, or both. At the very least, it was a good match of personalities.

"This definitely fits what we found at the scene," Fawcett

said once she finished skimming the file, "but surely you can't think all of these cases are related. The timeline is crazy."

"We think we've got a copycat killer, possible a younger relative or close associate of the prior killer—perhaps even killers. We're hoping the advances in modern crime scene investigation and forensics will help us understand how it was perpetrated, which we can use to find the killer," Wilson explained.

Huertas politely harrumphed. "That's a long stretch."

"It is," Wilson admitted, "but you have to agree that the state of the bodies is unique and their similarities over such long stretches of time suggests a connection. Otherwise, what we have is a series of unrelated deaths that just happen to end in butterflies. That doesn't sit right with me."

Fawcett grunted her reluctant agreement as she closed the file. "It's thin, but I think it's the right kind of thin. Where would you like to go first?"

Wilson closed his attaché. "I think it would be best if I saw where the body was found."

LA traffic lived up to its reputation, but they got there eventually. The atrocious gridlock was only one of the reasons Wilson didn't care for LA. For someplace with so much natural beauty, the city itself was completely devoid of substance, built entirely on artifice. While that appealed to some, he didn't care for it, but he basked in the good weather nonetheless.

Wilson took his own vehicle to spare himself any more of

Huertas's small talk. When they stopped, he retrieved an aerial map from his briefcase to orient where he was before getting out. The majesty of the place didn't hit him until he got out of his car. It was an untamed swath of green sitting high above the sprawling concrete jungle of LA. The string of clouds were highlighted with the vibrant colors of sunset—the only upside of the air pollution. The satellite pictures gave him a good idea of the lay of the land, but they never quite had the same impact as standing there in real life.

"What an odd place to find in the middle of one of the biggest cities in the world," Wilson said as he admired the view from the small parking lot of the Kenneth Hahn State Recreational Area. "Is that an oil field across the highway?"

Fawcett smiled at his admiration. She was LA born and raised, and it was always gratifying to hear someone else fall victim to its charms. "Indeed. That's the Inglewood Oil Field. They've been pulling oil out of here since the 1920s. The park's only been here since the '80s."

The senior detective started up the paved path. "We better get going if we want to make the most of what's left of the light," she remarked. On the ascent, the younger detective tried again, this time sticking to safe topics like the weather, but Wilson's silence absorbed the chatter until it ceased.

As they crested the adjacent hill, Wilson noted the small trees and scrub. There was a lot of natural cover. It'd be easy to walk around without being seen. About halfway up, Fawcett broke the silence. "We found the body right over here."

She motioned to the right and they veered onto a dirt path. The crime scene tape had been removed and there was still the odd butterfly flitting about the area. Wilson sniffed and there was a sweetness to the air. With the state of decomposition in the pictures, the place should still have the lingering hint of rotting flesh, even with a good airing out.

Fawcett stepped in front of a small concrete and wood pavilion whose top was lined with shaped concrete painted to look like the Spanish-style roofs common to LA. It was erected to provide a place for the less-athletic to rest in the shade on the ascent, but it could also provide cover for an attacker.

"What was the precise orientation of the body?" Wilson asked. There weren't enough detail in the picture for him to orient the body in his mind's eye and unlike the TV shows, they don't outline them in chalk.

Fawcett pointed to a section of the dirt path about forty feet past the pavilion. "The head was pointing toward the structure, face down."

Wilson pulled out an aerial printout from his inner jacket pocket. "Unless I'm mistaken, we're on *this* path," he said, holding the tip of his pen on a line abutting a neighborhood and the pavilion. The detectives concurred.

Fawcett's phone rang as Wilson formulated a plan. He'd need to salt once he had some privacy, and the adjacent neighborhood would have street parking for inconspicuous access to this section of the park if he couldn't shake the cops.

"Good news. Dr. Throckmorton will be performing the autopsy tomorrow morning and he's agreed to let you observe. Be at the morgue at 8:30 sharp," she relayed the message and put away her phone.

"Excellent. Thank you for arranging it," Wilson said politely. "I'm sure your team was more than thorough, but I'd like to spend some time walking the trails for myself. Helps me think."

"Would you like an escort?" she asked Wilson, and Huertas flashed her a look. *Please don't make me babysit him.*

"I should be fine. I've got this"—he held up the map in his hand—"and my rental has GPS."

"Then have a good walk and a good night, Special Agent Wilson," she replied with a slight nod of the head. "You coming, Huertas?"

"Right behind you, boss," he chimed and scurried down the hill before Wilson could change his mind.

"He's as cuddly as a cactus," Huertas commented when they were back on the paved path.

She shrugged. "He's here for work, not to make friends."

"It's not an either/or," he replied.

"It's also doesn't have to be both," she countered. They called it a draw and got back in their car.

Meanwhile, Wilson took a seat under the pavilion and pulled out his saltcaster, which looked like a vape pen to the uninitiated. He took off his tie and undid the top two buttons of his shirt; he was just another guy enjoying the scenery after a long day at work. When the coast was clear, he rotated the end of the tube until the notches lined up and blew out a dusting of fine salt.

Got you, he thought triumphantly as the grains started moving. It didn't take long, which meant some big magic happened here not too long ago. His victory was short-lived when a pattern finally emerged. He didn't recognize the magical signature, but he knew enough to interpret the major features: fae. It was starting to make sense: the scenery, the butterflies, the smell.

Wilson took a picture and sent it directly to Chloe and Dot, bypassing the second-floor analysts. He took to his feet and kicked the salt to disperse the residual magic. If he hadn't already come in as FBI, he could have broken into the morgue tonight, but that was the tradeoff. As Special Agent Wilson, he was going to get access and local assistance, but it had to be within their procedures.

On the off chance that the detectives were still in the parking lot, Wilson elected to walk the trail. The smell faded as he walked away from the pavilion, but it still bugged him. There was something vaguely familiar about the odor, but he couldn't place it. Contrary to Detective Huertas's turn of phrase, it wasn't roses, but it was definitely floral. He'd smelled it before, but he could not say where or when.

It was not quite dark when Wilson returned to his car. Below him, the lights of city were just starting to sparkle. From this perspective, LA didn't seem all bad. It was a nice park, if a bit dry.

Chapter Five

Los Angeles, California, USA
4th of March, 8:23 a.m. (GMT-8)

Wilson followed the hallway to a pair of double doors, where he could see through the windows that a white-coated man had already begun the autopsy. Wilson double-checked the time to make sure it wasn't yet 8:30 a.m. He was puzzled—Detective Fawcett didn't seem the type to get the time wrong. He entered the suite, suspicions raised.

Dr. Aldis Throckmorton was a tall lean man in his late forties. He had that tanned look of too many years spent in the sun. His sandy brown hair had rogue gray in the mix, and there was an effortlessness in his pearly smile. If he wasn't wearing protective gear with a liver in his hands, Wilson would have pegged him for a tennis instructor.

"Good morning. You must be Special Agent Wilson. Detective Fawcett said you'd be joining me this morning. I have to say, not many have the stomach to watch me work," the ME greeted him. "Liver, 1823 grams," he said aloud before returning it to its stainless steel basin and turning off the recorder.

"Thought I would spare you the grizzly bits, but here you are early. No matter. I'll be done shortly. He was a mess to clean up, but we've got him ship-shape now," the ME said cheerfully.

"Him?" Wilson repeated.

"Meet Tyler Adkins, a twenty-nine-year-old delivery driver. In his youth, Mr. Adkins spent three years as a guest of the California State Prison for assault and battery and had some work done on his teeth while serving his sentence, which is why we were able to identify him by dental records so quickly," Throckmorton spoke as he started putting the organs back into place.

"And the smell?" Wilson asked. He'd been around more than his fair share of dead bodies but none of them smelled like this. It was like someone had stuffed Adkins with potpourri—heavily floral with strong vanilla notes. It was definitely what he'd smelled at the crime scene, but more concentrated

The ME turned with a threaded needle in hand. "That, Special Agent Wilson, is the smell of butterfly sex." He started sewing while he talked. "Pheromones, to be more precise, but not the active ingredients, mind you. Humans can't smell those," he joked. "I had the lab rush the results once we heard you were coming."

Wilson moved closer to the table, but kept a respectful distance. "Thanks for that."

"Strange, this one. Look at the advanced decomposition," he said, knocking an elbow toward the pruned and putrid exterior. “But not the organs. Barely dead a day, if I had to guess,” he insisted as he sealed up the pericardial sac. “And no stink of it to be found! Not that I’m complaining, mind you. I’d rather smell the flowers than my normal daily bouquet,” he looked up and smiled at Wilson. There was a twinkle in his piercing green eyes. “But that’s why you’re here, right?”

Wilson found his comment and eye contact overly familiar, but chalked it up to LA. “We’re trying to see if this fits a pattern of previous murders. So far, it does. Beside the smell and bizarre decomposition pattern, have you found anything else of note?”

Throckmorton put aside his needle and thread and motioned to a box of disposable gloves on the wall. “You’ll want to grab a pair of those,” he assured Wilson as he approached the victim’s head.

The ME walked to the end of the table and harshly pulled the cadaver’s neck toward the chest. It sounded like a walnut cracking. “See this?” he said, pointing to something at the base of the skull.” Wilson, newly gloved, approached and looked at the putrefying skin underneath the doctor’s fingers. “It’s hard to see, what with the decomp, but it’s there.”

Wilson bent over and got in close. He ran a gloved finger over it just to make sure, but there was no doubt. It was an acquisitionist’s mark. It was azure blue and no bigger than a penny, but the sigil was plain as day.

Acquisitionists were humans enslaved by the fae and tasked to perform a discrete errand. The mark was magical in nature, compelling spirit-of-the-law obedience under threat of pain and eventual death. They were usually the result of a bad bargain or an encounter that had gone wrong, but once the task was done, the mark faded. Few were in place after a year, which meant that Adkins had somehow encountered fae and probably within the past twelve months.

Wilson ran through the possibilities, none of which he liked. If it occurred in the mortal realm, someone had summoned a faerie that had gotten out or a powerful faerie crossed over on its own. It was easy enough to bump into the fae in the Magh Meall, but that begged the question of how Adkins could have gotten into the middle lands.

While Wilson mulled, Throckmorton returned to his stitching. "I would say it's a tattoo, but it looks like it's been seared into the flesh. But it couldn't have been a brand because of the color. All together quite a puzzle, wouldn't you say?"

"Quite," Wilson tersely agreed while he took off his gloves.

"But there is nothing simple about the stamp of the touched, is there?" the ME asked without looking up.

Wilson immediately summoned his will. *Think, think, think...*

Throckmorton's nostrils flared and he took a submissive posture, both physically and metaphysically. He immediate put his hands up, palms forward, and his will rolled up like a pill bug that had been poked with a stick. "Stay cool, stay cool. I'm not a threat. I'm your friend. Who do you think tipped you off?"

Wilson ran his will over Throckmorton. His defenses were puny at best, but Wilson still kept his cards close to the chest. "And why would you do that?"

"Just doing my civic duty. As soon as I caught a whiff of this on my docket, I phoned it higher up. I got a nose for these things," he said, wiggling the tip of his nostrils like Samantha from *Bewitched*.

Wilson withdrew his projection without dismissing it. He had been in and out of morgues, hospitals, and police stations for years, but he'd yet to meet a practitioner in any of them. They weren't jobs that typically attracted the magically talented because, bluntly, they were entirely too thankless and underpaid.

The ME was an unknown factor. The Mine routinely did checks on everyone an agent was expected to interact with on a mission, and they would have warned Wilson if Throckmorton was on their radar. Wilson shifted his attention to getting as much information on him as possible.

"It appears you're a man of many talents," he said flatly, giving nothing away.

"I dabble," Throckmorton said, slowly lowering his arms and resuming his normal posture.

"Dabbling's dangerous."

"I *carefully* dabble," he qualified. "I mostly just do the job that I like and give a little extra push here and there, whenever

I want a change of scenery or a new opportunity." He flashed a smile. "I've never failed an interview, if you know what I mean."

Wilson nodded.

"I've heard about you guys. FBI. Practitioners. Never could find you no matter how hard I looked. Suppose that's the point, though. What good is a secret organization if you're easy to find. Am I right?" He nervously laughed. Wilson neither confirmed or denied his suspicions and waited silent and stone-faced for the doctor's nerves to get the better of him.

"What I'm saying is…I have abilities that might be useful to your organization. I've been in forensics my whole life, and coupled with my other talents, I could be flown in and take over an autopsy for strange cases such as Mr. Adkins," the ME made his pitch.

"And…?" Wilson uttered without moving his face.

Throckmorton beamed at that single syllable "And, for instance, I can tell you this guy didn't know how to use magic."

"How do you know that?" Wilson allowed him to explain.

"I've learned how to smell magic after burning out my nostrils doing a series of autopsies on dead practitioners. Now, I can do it almost unconsciously. I smelled you out as soon as you walked in the door," he added with conviction.

Wilson took a harder look at Throckmorton. There was something familiar about him now that his carefree SoCal veneer had vanished. He mentally turned back the clock a few years, darkened the hair, shortened the cut, removed the glasses, and turned his green eyes brown. "Ever worked as an ME in El Paso?" he inquired. There'd been a coven of witches that ended up frying themselves via a poorly executed summoning attempt. It had been one of Wilson's first assignments.

Throckmorton smiled wide. "You didn't recognize me at first, did you? I've got a forgettable face, which is worthless in Hollywood but it's gotta come in handy in your line of work."

"Interesting proposal, Dr. Throckmorton, but we both have enough on the table already, don't you think?" Wilson tilted his head at the gaping chest cavity that hadn't been stitched closed.

Throckmorton played it cool. "Right, one case at a time." He rubbed his gloved hands together in the universal sign of getting back to work. "What can I do for you now?"

Wilson thought for a second. "Best thing would be to leave me alone with the body for a bit."

"Yeah, sure, no problem," he immediately replied as he removed his gloves and washed up at the sink. "I could use a restroom break and another cup of coffee. That would take me at least five minutes," he suggested.

"Maybe even ten," Wilson threw it out there.

The ME dried off his hands. "Could be." He winked and tapped the side of his nose. "The butterflies that came in with the body are in those jars on the side table," he added, trying to be helpful. "I'll be filing my report in about an hour and I'm sure it'll be passed on to you by our friends at the LAPD. One thing I'd like to draw your attention to is that there weren't any other insects on the body."

"No bugs?" Wilson asked incredulously. A body in that state of decomposition should be covered with various insects picking up an easy meal.

"Not one. There were none in the soil *under* the body, either."

"So it was dumped?"

"That's going to be my official take. But, you know, with things being what they are, that's not necessarily the case."

Wilson nodded.

"Nice meeting you, Special Agent Wilson, and don't forget to pass my request up the chain of command."

"Enjoy your coffee, Dr. Throckmorton," Wilson dismissed him and the ME finally stepped out with a quick wave of the hand.

He's got chutzpah, Wilson thought to himself as he pulled out his vape pen and pressed the button for the electrical disruptor. It was good for ten meters, enough to cover the entire room, including any hidden cameras Throckmorton might have put into place.

He salt-casted under the corpse and under the computer station where he-who-was-called-Throckmorton worked—the name had to be a fake; he couldn't remember the name the ME used in El Paso, but he knew it wasn't Throckmorton. There were two distinct signatures under the corpse: the first matched the crime scene and the second matched the cast under the computers. Wilson took pictures and swept up the salt with a small broom he found in one of the closets. He helped himself to a butterfly as well as a clipping of Adkins' hair. Once he was finished, he toggled off the electric jammer and made his exit. *Best to let him sweat*, Wilson thought.

Once he was back in his car, he sent the magical signatures to the Mine along with a report on the doctor and his unusual proposition. It wouldn't take the analysts long to hunt down the name of the ME on the El Paso case. There were plenty of reasons people changed their name and appearance, but for Throckmorton's sake, Wilson hoped getting in magical trouble wasn't one of them. Then, he pulled up the last known address of the deceased to see if he could figure out how a delivery driver who was supposedly not a practitioner ended up with an acquisition mark.

Chapter Six

Lynwood, California, USA
4th of March, 10:08 a.m. (GMT-8)

Tyler Adkins lived alone in a studio apartment in the shabbier part of neighboring Lynwood, a stone's throw away from Compton. The streets and their occupants got progressively rougher as Wilson neared his destination. The average age of the automobiles soared as he pulled into the parking lot of a long single-row apartment complex. The front office advertised "Weekly Rates" and he spotted an ancient security camera as he drove past. It had been busted so long ago that rust had taken most of it.

He parked in the rear under one of the shattered lamps to avoid detection. There were no squad cars in sight and with any luck, he would be in and out of Adkins's apartment before LAPD had even notified the family. Should he be interrupted, his FBI badge would provide enough cover to uniforms and civilians alike.

Number twenty-four was on the second floor, and Wilson hurriedly took the stairs, palming his lock picks for a speedy entry. He checked for any magical wards before establishing physical contact. Finding none, he deftly placed the picks into the lock. Cheap apartment deadbolts were all alike and in less than twenty seconds, he let himself in.

The interior was as run down as the exterior. The popcorn-textured walls could have used a new coat of paint and the carpet was well worn and pad thin. The furniture was sparse and secondhand, but there were small signs that its occupant had taken care of it to the best of his ability. Whatever Tyler Adkins might have been, he had also been neat and organized, which made Wilson's job easier.

The first thing he did was pull out his saltcaster and salt the room. He had no reason to doubt Throckmorton's assessment that Adkins wasn't a practitioner, but good tradecraft dictated confirmation. He gloved up while he waited for the enchanted grains to pick up any magical residue. Within a minute, the salt finished its dance. When it settled into a single pattern, a smug grin broke across Wilson's normally impassive face. The magical signature was definitely fae and distinctly different from the one at the crime scene. This one Wilson immediately recognized: Dökkálfar.

The Dökkálfar were subterranean dark elves that resided in the Magh Meall—the buffer zone between the Land of Fae and the mortal realm. They were originally one of the seven royal fae families collectively known as the Tuatha Dé Danann, but something happened sixteen hundred years ago and the whole clan was demoted from great house status and banished from the entire Land of Fae—not just from the demesne of the Tuatha Dé Danann known to mortals as Tír na nÓg. Additionally, the remaining six royal families trapped them into a single form that was sensitive to the purple-tinged light of the Magh Meall, forcing them underground and away from the warmth of the sun.

Wilson didn't know what transgression the Dökkálfar had committed, but their punishment didn't end there. All the lesser fae houses were permitted to wage open war upon the fallen great house; fae tradition dictated that the clan who eradicated the last of the Dökkálfar would become the new seventh great house. The six remaining royal houses were forbidden to intervene in any way, lest they undermine the honor of the injured party seeking justice. However, it would seem the Dökkálfar had some sympathizers among the Tuatha Dé Danann, as living underground offered a measure of protection from the ambitious lesser fae. Even now after centuries of open conflict, the war raged on without an end in sight.

The expulsion didn't just rock the Land of Fae and the middle lands; Chloe and Dot linked the fall of the Western Roman Empire to the fall of the Dökkálfar. The librarians hypothesized the Romans relied heavily upon the fallen house's aid, and without their support were left in dire straits as the dangers within and outside their borders persisted.

Wilson pulled out his phone and snapped a picture while he pondered the implications. The Dökkálfar didn't kill Adkins, but perhaps they were the ones that put the acquisitionist's mark on him. He always felt safer when he knew what he was dealing with, but their involvement raised more questions. If Adkins wasn't a practitioner of the arts, how did he come into contact with the dark elves? And what task or item did the disgraced house of fae want that required a human?

He rubbed his foot over the salt signature, dispersing the magic and grinding the fine particles into the carpet, and began his search in earnest. He hit all the usual hiding places with laser precision, looking for the things Adkins preferred to keep private. People liked to think of themselves as clever, but they were really quite predictable. He found the usual array of contraband and left it in place for the LAPD to find during their search, but there was nothing supernaturally suggestive.

Once he exhausted the secreted spaces, he looked for the clues hiding in plain sight. His diligence was rewarded when he found a crumpled receipt in the wastebasket in the bedroom: a paid-for-in-cash church trip voucher to Fairy Circle Farms Bed and Breakfast. He snapped a picture for later reference and put everything back the way he found it.

He locked the deadbolt behind him as he left the apartment and took his gloves off once he was back in his rental. He plugged the B&B's address into his phone. It was about ten miles inside of Sequoia National Forest and only a four hours' drive from his current location.

He mentally manipulated the facts, seeing which parts fit

together. Without being a practitioner, it was unlikely that Adkins had deliberately entered the Magh Meall, and while it wasn't impossible for the Dökkálfar to enter the mortal realm, it would have taken a considerable amount of energy for the hunted clan—unless either of them stumbled upon an active fairy circle.

Fairy circles were no more than rings of mushrooms, the fruiting body of the mycelium underneath—the vast majority of which were non-magical, despite their association with fairies in popular lore. However, some rings could last centuries, and it was these enduring fairy circles that occasionally became problematic. Over time, durable fairy rings could wend their way into the Magh Meall, creating a connection between the two realms. These active fairy circles were the germ of many a fairytale, and in the old days, it was how practitioners entered the middle lands before shortbread and thirteen o'clock.

The giant sequoias were old growth, so it wasn't unreasonable that one of the fairy rings within could be, too. Wilson checked the date of stay on the receipt to support his rudimentary theory: Adkins was there last weekend. He wasn't one to believe in coincidence and typed in a quick report and a request for information to the Mine once he'd made up his mind to follow his gut. If his hypothesis was a bust, it would only cost him a day and an eight-hour drive round trip.

He ignored the squeaks and squawks from his phone's GPS as he took a detour to his hotel to pick up his luggage and check out. Next, he left a message for Detective Fawcett, letting her know that he'd been called away but to keep him informed of any new developments. She seemed the dogged type and he didn't want to leave any dangling threads for her to pull, like the sudden disappearance of an FBI agent in her city.

He filled up at a gas station on his way out of town and walked the shelves for food and drink. The corner of his mouth upturned when he saw the ranch corn nuts. It was one of the perks of working alone—no one to lodge complaints about odiferous snacks. He paid in cash, uncertain how the Mine wanted to account for this jaunt.

He set up his playlist and strategically positioned everything for the long drive ahead of him. Then, he loosened his tie and pulled out his sunglasses. Within half an hour, the city was behind him and he took in the fresh air and the scenery. The scars of last year's wildfires were still visible, but life persisted with new growth peeking out from the charred remains.

He made a pit stop in Bakersfield to stretch his legs and get something more substantial to eat than corn nuts. Halfway through his sandwich, he got a message from the Mine: ALL CLEAR. He appreciated the clarity with which the Mine communicated, even when it was the more ominous heading: DANGER.

He opened the message in full and skimmed over the dossier on Fairy Circle Farms Bed and Breakfast, a collection of private cabins located on fifty acres of land that stretched out behind the village of Ponderosa. The files contained information on the establishment itself, the owner's and manager's names, and a background check and financials on both. The analysts deemed it completely legitimate and—more to Wilson's interest—non-magical as of the last fairy circle check.

Magically active fairy rings were automatically de-linked and the area would be checked periodically for reactivation—an ounce of prevention was worth a pound of cure. Aurora had performed the last check two years ago because a decade earlier, a rogue dréwom—one of the animated tree people that dwelt in the Magh Meall—had crossed over via an active ring and attacked visitors of the national forest.

A lot can change in two years, Wilson wryly thought to himself as he chewed his ham and cheese. Two years ago, Alex was still dead, he'd never met Baba Yaga, and he didn't have a cat who could walk through walls. He read further to find instructions to go in as David Watson, Director of Acquisitions for Discretion Minerals. They'd already booked him a room.

A few hours later, Fairy Circle Farms Bed and Breakfast peeked out of the pines at the end of the scenic Western Divide Highway that ran North-South through the western part of Sequoia National Forest. The B&B's position along the ridgeline separating two rushing watersheds offered its guests incredible views of the forest's giant namesakes.

Gravel crunched under his tires as he pulled into the parking spot in front of the main lodge. It was a social focal point where guests checked in and out, guided tours gathered, and it was also the entry into the underground caves where they grew cloud mushrooms, a special local variety that was originally cultivated in the forest.

After he checked in and got the keys to his cabin, Wilson grabbed a folded pamphlet containing the map of the nature trails in the area as well as the locations of all the known fairy circles. Normally he wouldn't put much stock in tourist literature, but given the draw of the place was the fungi, anything that could remotely pass as a fairy ring would be hailed as an attraction.

There were thirteen indicated on the brochure's map, and Wilson guessed that he would have to cover about eight or ten miles to visit them all. He checked the time on his Girard-Perregaux; at least he had several hours of daylight left.

He hit the trails as soon as he was out of his dress clothes and into his running gear, trenching tool carefully hidden until he was well out of sight from the main lodge. The gravel from the parking lot covered the first couple of hundred feet, but the path quickly gave way to hard-packed earth covered with a soft blanket of pine needles. It made for excellent running, almost as good as a padded stadium track.

Before Avalon, running held no interest for Wilson. He'd preferred boxing or circuit training for cardio, and if he had to work on his endurance and speed, he'd happily hop on a treadmill. But after his stay in the endless rolling green hills, he totally understood why people ran and he could now go long stretches without tiring. It was just one of the many changes he'd discovered PA: Post Avalon. His footfalls fell into a rhythm with his steady breaths, and his lungs filled with the musky scent specific to old coniferous forests.

He was just getting into his stride when he came upon a small plaque that said this was where the first ring should be, but all that was there were a few mushrooms in an arc among the towering giants. Incomplete rings were no danger and Wilson struck it off his list. The next two were also arcs but the fourth was more promising.

Encircling a massive ponderosa pine was a ring of brown-capped mushrooms with white speckles. Wilson summoned his will—*think, think, think...*—and gingerly touched the edge of the circle with a thin thread of his magic. He braced himself for sparks, like when a negative and positive line made contact, but there was nothing. He made note of the complete circle of mundane mushrooms for the Mine's files and moved on.

He continued in that fashion, driven by the desire to hit all the circles before sunset. The last thing he wanted was to stumble onto an active fairy circle at night. He was at the apex of his run when he saw the placard for the eleventh fairy circle. This one was off the main trail, and he followed a well-worn footpath to a clearing that ended in a wide fairy circle almost ten feet across. In its center were remnants of a small fire despite the numerous signs prohibiting such behavior. Wilson sighed—people really were the worst. When he touched his will against it, he felt a metaphysical shock, the arcane equivalent of rubbing socked feet against carpet and touching another person.

Wilson walked around it, carefully tapping his will against it from all angles until there was no doubt—he'd found a magically active fairy circle. He salt-casted outside the perimeter and breathed a little easier when there was no trace of Dökkálfar. He still had to destroy the fairy ring, but at least he didn't have to hunt down dark elves in the mortal realm.

He unfolded his trenching tool and cut a single shallow trench, breaking the circle by uprooting a cluster of mushrooms. He threw out another line of will confirmed that it was inert. That would stop any more humans from stumbling into the middle lands until he could completely sever the connection.

He made notes on his map and continued on his circuit, hitting the final two fairy rings on the way back to his cabin. Just because he found one didn't mean there weren't more. Plus, he needed to find a good secluded place to finish the job tomorrow.

Chapter Seven

Three Rivers, California, USA
5th of March, 9:30 a.m. (GMT-8)

Wilson strode the six aisles of what passed as a grocery store in Three Rivers, stocking up on provisions for his trip into the Magh Meall. *In all matters, before beginning, a diligent preparation should be made*, he mentally quoted Cicero as he assessed his options.

The Three Rivers Market may have been lacking in Highland shortbread, but it did have pecan sandies. Americans didn't regard it as shortbread, but it was in the same cookie spirit which was close enough for the fae. He added a box to his shopping basket and couldn't help the wry smirk that escaped. It would infuriate the vain and haughty fae that the Keebler elf was a prevalent representation of their kind in his part of the mortal realm.

He munched down on two sandwiches, a banana, and espresso in a can before setting out on the trail, this time walking. The last two fairy circles he'd checked yesterday were duds, so all he had to do was sever the connection from the Magh Meall on the eleventh ring and he could make his way back to LA. He'd also found a secluded spot out of sight from the trails roughly a hundred yards from the fairy ring in question.

When he arrived at his secluded destination, he used his trenching tool to cut a shallow circle into the piney soil just large enough for him to sit within. He placed each of the four candles in the cardinal directions and crumbled the sandies in a loose line around the interior of the trench, popping any large pecan pieces into his mouth along the way. He positioned his trusty 1950's Bucherer traveling alarm clock opposite him and quickly ate the remaining two sandwiches he'd bought this morning. He wasn't particularly hungry, but there would be no eating or drinking once he entered the Magh Meall. He washed it down with a bottle of water and assumed a meditative position as the clock face read 11:55.

Wilson gathered his will and voiced a simple supplicating chant to the fae, asking them to allow a poor mortal into the middle lands. When the Swiss clock chimed out twelve, he ended the chant, closed his eyes, and extended his will, winding it around the circle until it was dense and thick like the wool yarn of a baseball. Then he entered his hour of meditation.

As always, it was the smell that let him know he'd crossed over. It was hard to explain its crisp purity to anyone that hadn't been to the Magh Meall. Even the dirt—which was the most authentic dirt one had ever wafted—smelled clean. He was so taken with aroma that it didn't register that he hadn't heard the clock chime thirteen until he opened his eyes and saw it was only 12:55.

What the hell…? How am I five minutes early? His hindbrain flared and he drew his will and his Glock, sweeping the area without leaving the anchor of the circle. Even the trees were taller and more majestic, and their shifting canopy let ribbons of purple-tinged light pass through their gaps. While he found no threat, Wilson waited in the circle until the Bucherer chimed thirteen. It was a long five minutes, even by Magh Meall standards where time passed differently.

Once he felt secure, he holstered his weapon. Five minutes early was just another thing to add to the list of PA changes. It wasn't really any weirder than any of the others, but he found it more unnerving because of the departure from the norm. Going into the Magh Meall was something he'd done many times, and never once had he arrived a *second* earlier than thirteen o'clock.

He stepped out of his circle with his trenching tool in hand and made his way to the fairy circle. From this side, it was truly a thing of beauty. The powered ring sparkled and glittered and each constituent mushroom was its own shiny color, as if they were made of chromed metal. Periodically, bits of tinkling music floated across, attracting anything nearby. Magic longed to be used and fairy rings were no exception.

Wilson carefully observed the fairy circle and tested it remotely with an extended line of will. When nothing untoward happened, he unfolded the trencher and uprooted the first cluster of many. Breaking the line in the mortal realm ended the multi-world connection, but the portal would quickly reconnect if he did not address the Magh Meall side. As the metal tore into the earth, the displaced mushrooms quickly lost their shine and then their color. By the time he was halfway through the circle, the first batch had already started to rot.

"I wish you wouldn't do that," a feminine voice called out from the nearby tree line.

Wilson dropped his shovel and drew his Glock in one smooth motion as he rolled out of the ring. He was in firing position faster than humanly possible. The distant part of his mind that wasn't focused on the potential threat calmly noted that his training with Liu *was* paying off.

Leaning against one the trees was an intensely attractive nude woman. Her skin was tree-bark brown and her silky hair a deep pine green. Her shoulders were squared and one of her hands was clenched into a fist.

Hamadryad, Wilson immediately identified the figure and a series of factoids flooded his brain as he accessed what he knew of them. Like all fae, they were incredibly beautiful, and from Wilson's perspective, the library's description of their allure didn't do this one justice. They were mercurial but slightly easier to reason with due to their affinity with trees. Among the flighty fae, they were considered grounded and sensible. They were generally neutral actors, but fierce when made an enemy.

Wilson holstered the Glock and took a submissive posture that still allowed him some maneuverability. "My apologies, fair dryad, but I must prevent any from crossing over. One of my kind has already died because of the ring," he replied politely.

"But your kind dies so quickly anyway, and the beauty of the ring could last forever," she pointed out petulantly. Small thorns grew over her skin and extended into two-inch long spikes whose tips glistened with something unpleasant.

Wilson didn't like where this was heading and tried a different approach. "What if I replaced some of the beauty without the danger to my kind?"

She cocked her head to one side. She rarely interacted with mortals and their usual propositions were much baser than what this little man was offering. She stilled her defenses but didn't dismiss them. "How so?"

Wilson kept his posture and chose his words carefully—she wouldn't attack him as long as he intrigued her. "I'm not like most of my kind. I can make things. I could show you, if you would allow me."

She didn't expect such manners from such an ugly thing. It amused her. "You may," she granted him permission to move.

Wilson retrieved the mushroom he'd just pulled up and filled it with his will. Its color stopped draining and slowly returned to how it was just prior to its harvest, although he could not return its luster. He metaphysically tied it off, capturing the magic within the fungus like air in an inflated balloon.

He offered it to her as a sign of friendship in the manner Moncrief had instructed him long ago. The hamadryad clapped her hands and giggled with delight. She held out her hands, indicating that Wilson should come closer and deliver his gift. It wasn't until he tried to rise and saw spots in his vision that he realized how draining the spell was. Transmutation wasn't in his usual wheelhouse as it had made him high as a kite before Avalon. The arts in the Magh Meall might be karma free but they still required effort on the caster's part, and the less experienced, the more the effort.

He recovered quickly and her thorns diminished with each step. By the time he deposited the vibrant canary yellow mushroom into her open palms, they were little more than prominent bumps on her barky skin. She brought it right up to her black eyes, staring at it from barely an inch away. In the scrutiny of her gaze, she found it worthy, but just. "And how long will *this* last?" she asked sharply.

Wilson took a step back before answering. "As long as I do. I cannot make it last longer."

She frowned; mortals were not known for being long lived. Still, now she could take it with her, which counted for something. In a singular sweep on her hand, she pushed the mushroom into her bosom for safekeeping. "Make me more pretty mushrooms, human!" she demanded.

Seeing the chance to bargain, Wilson made a suggestion, "I'll make you one for every question you truthfully answer for me about the circle." As he spoke, he laced his words with his will, extending the option of a binding oath.

The hamadryad considered his proposal. Tiny branches grew and retracted from her head. "Two per question," she countered.

Wilson paused for theatrics; he did not want her to know how much he valued the information. He took the time to phrase his questions to require as few as possible. When he had it down to two, he finally replied. "Agreed."

A silver thread of will extruded from the hamadryad's chest and it briefly entangled with Wilson's, completing the esoteric handshake that bound the two parties to the terms of the agreement.

"My first question is: what do you know about any Dökkálfar who have approached the circle or are within the nearby environs?" Wilson began.

She laughed and it sounded like a lilting birdsong carried over the rustle of leaves in a light breeze. While fae held the spirit of the law over the letter of the law, that didn't stop them from bending the rules where they could for sport and advantage. They were mischievous by temperament and couldn't help but recognize and respect that in others. Getting two questions out of one was just the sort of thing a fae would do if given the chance.

"You *are* a maker, aren't you? I should not have expected

less," the dryad marveled. Wilson smiled and gave her little bow. The niceties were to be observed when interacting with fae.

She straightened up—fulfilling oaths was serious business—and in so doing, her bosom and curves became more pronounced. "Yes, I have seen Dökkálfar at the circle and know of a cave from which they enter and exit."

"Thank you for the information, fair dryad," Wilson said before returning to the circle, cutting down two mushrooms, and sealing in their beauty—one candy apple red and the other azure. He was noticeably winded by the effort but brought them to her nonetheless. She accepted them and pressed them into the chest.

"Have you more questions?" she asked, hoping to add to her incipient collection.

"I have one more, but I must rest before the asking," he replied, catching his breath while taking a knee.

"Certainly," she said, dropping to her haunches in a squat. She did not mind waiting for more pretties. As she waited, she was absolutely still. Unlike mortals, she didn't need to draw breath, blink, or fidget to remind herself she was alive. She simply was.

When Wilson felt up to the task of making more, he culled two mushrooms, one by one, capturing their brilliant hues. He presented them to the dryad and waited for her to take them before voicing his next question.

When the last stem disappeared into her barky chest, he spoke. “Could you show me where the cave entrance you spoke of is located?” A Cheshire grin of appreciation spread across her striking face. She had already accepted the mushrooms and was bound to answer the question honestly.

“That’s not really a question; it is a request for an action,” she responded coyly, “but I can see you have completely tired yourself while I have only answered questions. Let me be fair in this, our bargain. I will take you there if you’d like.”

Wilson nodded and before he could ask for more time to muster his energy, she picked him up in her arms like a child, growing to accommodate his size until she was at least twelve feet tall. She held him tightly against her ample bosom and her skin was warm and soft despite being made of bark. *This is definitely better than being carried in Mau’s mouth,* he thought to himself as she passed through the woods. Her stride was long, making short work of the quarter-mile trip to the edge of a small drop-off.

She set him down on the ground and pointed to a dark spot on the other side of the shallow valley. “That is where the dark elves came from.”

Wilson oriented himself and picked out unique features should he need to return. While he still didn’t know who killed Tyler Adkins, he had more clarity on at least one of the players. If the butterfly deaths were a result of rare dark elf involvement with the mortal world, there was no need to do more. With the fairy circle broken on both sides, the Dökkálfar weren't going anywhere anytime soon, and a few murders every thirty or forty years wasn't worth risking a full assault on the fallen house. They were outcasts, but they were still very powerful fae. He was content to wait and see if any more butterfly-covered corpses appeared before escalating.

"It occurs to me," the hamadryad broke his train of thought, "that if you stayed, you could make me more pretties and they would last longer." The dryad was back to human-sized and held a cluster of luscious ripe red berries in her hands.

Wilson's brain squirmed, simultaneously aroused and repulsed at the invitation, but the mild smile on his face remained unchanged. Some men would jump at the chance to be with a dryad and pass their days in the endless summer of the Magh Meall, blissfully free of whatever obligations and responsibilities they had in the mortal realm. However, Wilson knew better.

His mind churned, looking for the best way to decline without angering her. "It is a tempting thought," he started, "but I have oaths to keep in my realm." He could tell she was not accustomed to being told no, but he knew his gamble had paid off when she merely pouted as the berries reabsorbed back into her hands. If there was anyone who understood the sanctity of an oath, it was the fae.

"What a pity. You showed such promise," she flippantly lamented.

"But if you guide me back to the fairy circle, I will make one last mushroom for you, the large plump purple one," he replied. She nodded in agreement and turned on her heels, and Wilson picked up the pace, following closely behind her.

Chapter Eight

Detroit, Michigan, USA
9th of March, 3:53 a.m. (GMT-5)

A cold chill billowed around of the heavy coat of Detective Flint Ironstag. The furry frill of the hood did little to soften his chiseled jaw and hard eyes. The late winter morning pressed down on the large man—just another burden heaped upon many to be borne on his broad shoulders. There wasn't anything like Detroit at the end of winter. As the season grew long in the tooth, it turned cranky and mean; a late frigid cold snap was prone to shank you like an inmate in a prison yard while you're looking at the sky and dreaming of spring.

He hated early morning calls, not that midday or evening calls brought better news, but there was something singularly soul sucking about being pulled out of one's warm bed to investigate a crime. They deserved a special place in hell as far as he was concerned. They reminded him of the personal cost of the constant pressure of his job. What he'd lost when work perpetually demanded his best. They were the reason his marriage had crumbled around him and why he'd lost his daughter to inattention and crack houses across the river in

Socialist Canada. He couldn't even stand the smell of maple syrup anymore.

Everyone talked about how tough the cops in New York or Chicago were, but they couldn't hold a candle to Detroit's boys in blue. It was a city that bred tough cops and winter was only the tip of the iceberg. How many black bears has your average Big Apple or Windy City cop gone toe to toe with? None, that's how many. Ironstag had faced down two in the last five years alone as well as a pack of coyotes. The food trash brought them into the city while the barren blighted spots gave them sanctuary. Animal control was nigh useless. They were always drunk, smoking weed, or filming that animal rescue show that brought in the big bucks that honest work didn't. No one was doling out that kind of green to Detroit PD. They had to *earn* their wages.

And that was exactly what Detective Ironstag was doing as he barreled his way through the crowd, eyes zeroed in on the crime scene tape fluttering in the wind. No matter the time of day, a crowd always gathered whenever a body was found. He passed through the perimeter held by the uniforms like a hot knife through butter and found his partner already on the scene.

Ironstag skipped over the pleasantries. "What do we got today, Murphy?"

The stout detective rose from his squat, joints creaking in the cold. "Another pretty popsicle," Murphy responded, his gruff voice bouncing off the frozen sides of the filthy alley. "Found an hour ago. Forensics isn't here yet."

He pointed down between two blue dumpsters for Ironstag's benefit. The bins were almost touching, battered and dented on all sides like two heavyweight boxers slogging it out in the final round. Nestled between them was a body.

She'd been a pretty girl before someone bashed her over the head. Her honey blonde hair was matted with blood, freeze-dried and crusted with flakes of snow collecting on the crimson. Ironstag couldn't keep the look of disgust off his face.

"Think she's a hooker?" Murphy asked, eyeing the large amount of exposed flesh. "An alley trick gone wrong?"

Ironstag had long become inured to his partner's cynicism, but the resemblance to his own daughter made this comment cut deep. She would have been about the same age, were she still alive. "You're old, Murphy. Everyone dresses like that now," he spat out with raw emotion.

Murphy shrugged defensively. He'd worked too many years, seen too many things to have empathy for the nightly dead. He would have never made it this long if he felt the full weight of their demise, and he only had a few years left before he would retire with a full pension.

"Excuse me for having ideas," he muttered under his steamy breath.

Ironstag crouched beside the body and, in a breach of protocol, closed the lids over the vacant silvery eyes. Her wide, symmetrical face was pale and smooth like a porcelain doll, and now just as cold in death. He stood abruptly and Murphy's portly form blurred as he looked down the alleyway toward the glaring lights of the squad cars. He pulled back the hood of his coat to get more air, revealing the hawkish, smooth-shaven head underneath. The cold sting brought him back to the matter at hand. "This never gets any easier," he dramatically uttered.

"—and CUT!" Amanda Priest, the director of *Cold Blue: Detroit* called out. "I think we got it, folks. Good job." In an instant, the site exploded in activity as everyone on the set resumed normal activity and voices raised to be heard. A few clapped and cheered, but it was unclear if they were moved by the performance or just happy it was the last shot of the morning.

"Andrew, get some clothes on Megan," Priest shouted over the din to one of her assistants. She knew the main actors on the show would have plenty of people fawning over them, but she remembered what it was like being the little guy before she fought her way into the director's seat. It wasn't that long ago that she was just a pretty corpse in a procedural.

A young man with a headset swooped in, depositing a thick insulated coat, socks, and footwear to the now-seated Megan Anderson. The chroma-keyed green mat was cushioned and heated like an electric blanket, but it could only do so much when she was nearly nude at below-freezing temperatures.

"Thanks, Andrew," Anderson said as she burrowed into her winter coat. She always made it a point to memorize everyone's name and to call them by it whenever possible. It was one of the first tricks she had learned—people liked the sound of their own name. Plus, it never hurt to make nice with the crew. They were the ones on the ground that kept a production going and she never knew which connections would help her find the next gig.

"Goddamn it's cold!" Lucius Green, the actor playing Flint Ironstag, cursed as he pulled his coat's hood back over his bald head. He snapped his fingers and had a warm cup of coffee in his hand within seconds. "Whose idea was it to film on location again?"

"You know we gotta keep doing it, Lucius," the director verbally smoothed over her star actor's ruffled feathers as he peacocked. "The city is one of the characters and the viewers love it."

The actor scowled. "People watch the show because of *me*, Amanda," he insisted as he slipped back into his native British accent. "And I'm tired of freezing my bollocks off for these ludicrous early morning takes."

Jake Beals, the actor playing Murphy, grabbed himself a hot cup of coffee from the craft services table. He knew his place in the hierarchy: an aging character actor with a face for radio. It was too early and cold for one of Green's soliloquies, and he cut his co-star off before he could remind everyone he used to do Shakespeare at the Royal. Again.

"*Someone* forgot his thermals today," Beals teased and the rest of the crew turned away before snickering. Green was a good actor, but he was far from what Beals would call "a good guy." Six out of ten times, he took the path of *most* resistance and didn't understand why no one sympathized with his plight.

"At least I have something to protect," Green shot back lamely. "When's the last time you've seen yours under that belly?"

Beals didn't miss a beat. "When you got a big tool, you need a big shed."

"You wish!" Green weakly sputtered and stormed off. In an argument, as Beals's father would have euphemized, Green was as sharp as a marble.

"Ladies and gentleman, give it up for the illustrious Lucius Green!" Beals feigned adoration and started clapping as the thespian climbed into the warm SUV an assistant kept nearby for refuge between takes.

Priest landed a swift swat on Beals's back. "Simmer down. The last thing any of us need is you fueling his persecution syndrome."

"Don't worry, Amanda. He'll pout and fuss but he'll always come back. No one remembers his King Lear, but everyone knows Flint Ironstag. You think his ego could walk away from that?" he reasoned but backed off all the same. He knew she was the reason he had this gig in the first place. Who could have guessed *Cold Blue: Detroit* would have made it six seasons?

Priest nodded to recognize his attempt at restraint before turning to address Anderson. "Not too cold, I hope. I promise the other scenes will be shot indoors."

Between the makeup and the cold, no one could discern the blush that came to Anderson's cheeks—*The director is talking to me*! "I knew what I was signing up for. I'm from Michigan," she answered, tying up her thick boots.

"See, that's a trooper. You were hardly wearing anything but Lucius is the one 'whinging' up a storm," Beals retorted.

Anderson wasn't sure of the social dynamic and stuck to stating the facts. "Well, it *is* cold." She didn't understand why that made the director grin as she walked away, but Anderson smiled back. That was the polite thing to do.

Beals huffed. "I'm not saying he's *wrong*. I'm just saying he's an asshole." That garnered an honest laugh from Anderson, which brightened his disposition considerably. She was an extremely attractive young lady and he'd gotten quite the good look at her during the multiple takes. This was her first and only scene with the stars of the show, and Beals was never one to waste an opportunity, regardless the age difference—or, to be more accurate, because of it.

"How'd you feel about catching some breakfast? I know a great place not far from here that's open," he asked casually.

It took her a while to process what was going on and wonder if she should say yes, so long that Beals was convinced he'd struck out. He was genuinely surprised when she answered with an awkward, "Looking like this?" She was wearing next to nothing under the coat and she still had her crime scene makeup on.

"Don't worry about it. This place is an authentic dive. Cheap as hell, frequented by drunks and the homeless, but it's got the best breakfast in town," he said with grizzled charm.

She pulled out her phone from her jacket pocket. "What's the name of this place?"

"The Hummingbird Grill—it's about half a mile away. It's the real deal. It's the kinda place you'd find Tom Waits trying to sober up in after a night he won't remember," he quipped but regretted his words when they failed to illicit a response. *Idiot, there is no way someone her age knows who the hell Tom Waits is.*

She finished typing with her thumbs and pulled up an address and directions. "Sounds good. Meet you there in about fifteen?" she suggested.

"We could go in my car?" he offered.

She smiled but her voice was firm. "Thanks, but I prefer to drive myself." That was one of many rules her father drilled into her as soon as it was clear to him how attractive she had become: always drive yourself. It didn't take her long to see his point. She always knew where she was, how she got there, how to get back, and more importantly, she could leave whenever *she* wanted. Related life skills like how to change a flat tire, do a basic check on the engine, and throw a punch were also covered.

Her silvery eyes sparkled in the bright set lights, and her resoluteness only drew Beals in further. "See you in fifteen."

Anderson made her way to the compact rental the show had provided and cranked the heater to full blast. She pulled out a knit sweater dress from her bag and draped it over her head, undoing her jacket enough to shimmy it down over her hips. With some aggressive wiping and face cream, she managed to get the bulk of the makeup off her face and her natural color was starting to come through. There wasn't much she could do about the fake blood crusted in her hair, but she managed to get a comb through it and part it the other way to hide most of it. She placed a few strategic bobby pins and the engine was finally warm by the time she was ready.

She flipped the heat to defrost and followed the maze of streets until she saw the "The Hummingbird Hotel & Grill" on the side of a four-story brick building. The sign was just the letters painted in red and filled in with full-sized red and pink lightbulbs, half of which weren't working. It looked like something from a state fair or vintage Vegas.

Finding parking was easy this early in the morning and she spotted Beals through the front window, waiting just inside the door for her. Going for breakfast with one of the show's co-stars seemed like a good idea fifteen minutes ago, but now she wasn't so sure. She took a deep breath and repeated what her mother always told her before she left the house as a teenager:

"Don't let anyone do anything that you don't want them to. And if they try—fight like hell, get away, and don't look back."

When she passed through the steel-barred glass door, all spontaneous conversation and movement stopped and a sea of dilated pupils stared at her. The cliental was exactly as promised. Some were clearly taking cover from the cold night, and two of the patrons were passed out with handwritten checks tucked under their arms. There was a crowded table sharing a single cup of warm coffee—all they could afford after they'd spent their money on more potent substances.

Beals looked up from his phone and caught sight of her transformed. "You changed," he uttered and immediately felt silly for stating the obvious. She was even lovelier than before despite the fact she was wearing significantly more clothing.

"I came to work in my own clothes," she replied matter-of-factly and took Beals's lead to the counter along the far wall. The lower half was tiled in pink craquelure glaze while the countertop was a thick pale pine, polished to a shine by many a dishtowel over the years.

The menu was a sign hanging on the wall covered with plastic lettering. In all caps, BREAKFAST only had six items with the prices listed à la carte: egg, toast, bacon, sausage, hash browns, pancakes. The letter "O" filled in for the occasional missing zero.

"How's my favorite fake Five-O?" the man behind the counter asked as they took two seats. He was old, wrinkled, and missing a few teeth, but it didn't dim his smile.

"Same old, same old, Willy," Beals congenially responded.

"Found another stiff in the neighborhood?" he inquired.

"In fact, I did. And she's sitting right here," he said with a little wave in Anderson's direction. Beals's introduction was all the excuse Willy Washington needed to give her the good stare he'd wanted to since she'd walked in.

"She don't look stiff, big man, but I'm feeling a bit myself," he said without the slightest bit of chagrin.

"It's probably arthritis," Anderson said directly. The two men went silent but the blonde didn't budget in her assertion. Given his age and the weather, it stood to reason. She wasn't sure why they suddenly burst into laughter, but she was used to not getting the joke. She waited for the humor to burn itself out and decided it was pancake sort of morning.

"What can I get you, sweetheart?" Washington asked after he finally regained his composure.

"Can you make those blueberry pancakes?" she asked.

"For you? No problem." He turned toward Beals. "Same as always?"

"You know it, Willy," the actor replied.

Washington topped off coffee cups on his way back to the kitchen to put in their orders, occasionally chuckling and muttering under his breath, "Probably arthritis!"

"This is...retro," Anderson made conversation and chose the most neutral yet true word she could think of.

Beals laughed but Anderson didn't mind. She might not always get why something was funny, but she could tell the difference between people being amused at something she said versus laughing at her. "It's only twenty years old but made to look older. The owner modeled it off the original Hummingbird Grill in New Orleans that had been around since the 1940s. I suppose that's why I like it so much. It was conceived with dirt under its nails."

Anderson crinkled her brow. She understood nostalgic throwback restaurants that glorified soda fountains and hamburger joints with checkered linoleum and shiny chrome, but this place was just dim, dark, and greasy. "What a strange thing to do."

Beals shrugged. "The guy who owns the place has a day job, some business-to-business tech company so he doesn't need the money. He occasionally pops in and pays for everyone's orders. People with a lot of money do strange things."

Anderson gave a noncommittal nod. She didn't know very many people with lots of money. "Do you do strange things with your money?"

Beals grinned. "Only if you consider inviting women half my age to the biggest dive in Detroit at four in the morning strange."

A small smile crept onto her pursed lips. "I think that qualifies as a little strange."

Beals pressed his luck a little further. "Good strange or bad strange?"

She paused and considered. "Good strange."

The food came fast and hot, and Anderson marveled at the size of her short stack. "You know, I've been eating here for years and he's never put blueberries in my pancakes," Beals teased her.

She looked sideways to his plate: fried eggs, bacon, and toast. "I thought you always order the same thing," she called him on his bluff as she poured a generous ribbon of syrup on her plate. This time, she understood why he was chuckling and the insight made her smile. Over breakfast, he asked her about growing up in Michigan, and she listened to him tell showbiz stories.

They were nearly done when Washington approached them again. "You need anything? I've got to take out the trash and won't be around for a few minutes."

"Little top up?" Anderson asked, pointing at her coffee.

"Sure thing, darling," he said with a wink and filled her cup, leaving just enough room for the cream and sugar.

"Don't forget mine, cupcake," Beals joked. Washington obliged with a sour look on his face before wandering off to the back of the restaurant.

She giggled. Beals was not traditionally handsome and he'd never be tall, but he was funny. She couldn't remember the last time she'd laughed this much with another person. She'd definitely had worse dates, if that's what this was.

She caught something out of the corner of her eye and all the color drained from her face. She turned around to make sure she wasn't seeing things. When she saw the figure standing on the sidewalk outside the Hummingbird, she sharply inhaled and held her breath. It felt like someone had pulled the rug out from under her and she was in free fall all over again.

Beals touched her arm. "What's wrong?" He followed her gaze, glued to a young man ominously standing outside. "You know him?"

"Darren," Anderson said with hesitation. Just saying his name was a strain. "An ex. He's not supposed to be this close to me."

He picked up on her phrasing. "Restraining order?"

She nodded.

Shit, Beals thought, taking the measure of the angry kid's face. He knew how this would play out in the world of *Cold Blue: Detroit* but this wasn't a TV show and he wasn't a gruff homicide detective. "You want me to call 911?"

She didn't have time to answer as the bell on the door chimed with Darren standing in the doorway.

Chapter Nine

Detroit, Michigan, USA
9th of March, 5:56 a.m. (GMT-5)

The flashing red and blue lights danced across the Hummingbird Hotel & Grill's sign. The entire section of sidewalk outside the entrance was cordoned off and traffic had been shunted down to one lane. But even at this early hour, there were commuters, and one by one, the cars passed at a reduced speed, catching a glimpse of what caused the commotion.

It was a rough part of town and no one was surprised to see a body covered with blue cloth on the sidewalk. Just another cold ending to someone they didn't know, a footnote when they relayed the events of the day to coworkers, friends, or family, but quickly forgotten in the rhythm of their routine.

Detective Jennifer Cerova raised the tape and walked onto the scene. She saw the body plain as day and noted the rippling under the sheet. It was a windy morning, but the waves weren't running across the surface. They seemed to bubble up from immediately below. Officer Thompson was rubbing his temples as he took Willy Washington's statement beside the alley. He flagged the detective down as soon as he saw her—no way was he going to be the one to relay Washington's story.

"You wanna repeat this for the detective, Mr. Washington?" he asked but it was really an order.

"I'm Detective Cerova, Mr. Washington," she introduced herself and presented her badge.

There was a slight delay before he responded. "You can just call me Willy. That's my name." The cigarette held loosely between his fingertips amplified the tremor in his hands. It wasn't just the cold that had him shaking.

Cerova softened her demeanor to put him at ease. "Okay Willy, would you tell me what happened?"

"Well, like I was saying, I was out back, dropping off the trash and sneaking in a smoke," he restarted his account. "I'm not supposed to do that, but I always make the rounds with the coffee pot right before. Night shift's always tight and I'm never gone longer than five minutes," he nervously added. His eyes kept going back to the body behind her.

"Sure," she voiced sympathetically at the extraneous information. She shifted her stance to block his view. "And then what happened?"

"So I'd dropped off the trash and was about halfway through my Pall Mall when I hear some screaming and then, bam!" he exclaimed and his face became animated. "There's this bright flash of light coming over the roof of the 'bird. A rainbow light, kind of like a firework, you know?" There was no way Cerova could have known what he was talking about but she nodded her head to keep him talking.

He flicked the string of ash off his cigarette before continuing. "And then everything goes dark and quiet. I stomp out my cig and go back inside. And when I get inside, everyone's asleep. George is curled up by the grill, sawing logs—"

"That's the cook, George Stanley," the uniformed officer clarified.

Washington nodded. "And when I look in the dining room, everyone was out—all curled up on the floor."

Cerova raised an eyebrow. "Asleep?"

"Yes ma'am, just like a titty baby after a suckle. And then I see Mr. Beals in the middle of the floor—"

"That's Jake Beals, the actor from *Cold Blue: Detroit*," Officer Thompson interrupted again.

"What's *Jake Beals* doing here?" Cerova asked incredulously and gestured to the environs to make her point.

"He likes the food," Washington said defensively. "May not be much to look at, but the food's cheap, good, and hot."

Cerova pantomimed contrition and Washington resumed his narrative. "I find him all splayed out in the middle of the floor instead of curled up by the counter and I try to wake him up, only he's not coming to. Then I get a glimpse of someone lying down on the sidewalk outside and I get a bad feeling in my gut—it's too cold to be lying down outside."

He paused and took a long drag off his dangling cigarette,

working up his courage to finish. "So I opened the door and found *that*, only without the butterflies. That came later." Washington's eyes darted once more in the general direction of the corpse under the blanket.

"The butterflies?" Cerova repeated to make sure she'd heard him correctly.

Officer Thompson nodded rapidly. "This is where things get weird," he said as an aside.

"I'm all ears," a crisp male voice came from up the street. "David Wilson, FBI," he introduced himself to Washington because he and Cerova were already acquainted. He was slimmer than the last time she'd seen him, but he wore the same impeccably tailored suit with cool precision. If he was on the scene, that meant there was something special about this case. They exchanged curt nods and Cerova coaxed the witness to finish.

"Please continue, Mr. Washing—Willy," she corrected herself midsentence.

"Um…okay," Washington said, trying to make sense of what came next. "When I found the body, it was all melty and black and purple. I wasn't sure what to do because it was well off…but it couldn't have been there for very long, you know? People had been coming in and out all night. Someone woulda said something, right? That's when I called 911 and I was about to go inside to check on the rest of the customers when it started to wiggle." Washington's face curled in disgust as he looked behind Cerova.

"Wiggle?" Cerova pressed gently.

"Yeah, it started to wiggle and these white blisters appeared and then they popped and all these little maggots crawled out. It was enough to make me toss my lunch." He pointed to a spot adjacent to the entrance to the Hummingbird to add credibility to his unbelievable tale. "I didn't want to be anywhere near it after that, so I went inside, woke everyone up, and by the time I looked out the window again, the damn thing was covered in butterflies." Thompson tilted his head toward the detective—*See? I wasn't lying. Weird.*

While the officers were coming to grips with Washington's account, Wilson stepped in. "When did you notice the smell—before or after the blisters popped?"

The smell? Cerova's inscrutable deep-set brown eyes bored into Wilson with none of the soft sympathy she reserved for getting information out of the skittish and breaking bad news to families. As they were the same height, he felt the weight of her stare and gave her a sideways glance that clearly said, *I'll explain later.*

Washington was looking up, trying to remember. It had been a long night. "After. It was pretty stinky when I first found him," he said slowly but his cadence picked up speed. "Look, I know this sounds crazy but I swear, I'm not on anything." He reached into his front pocket and pulled out a purple coin, "I've been sober for nine months now. Hand to God."

Cerova stepped in. It was still her crime scene. "I think we have what we need for the time being. Why don't you go inside and wait with the rest, Willy. The officers will get your information and we may have more questions later." She watched him shuffle off, giving the corpse a wide berth. Whatever was under there, it still had him spooked.

"You want to tell me what you know about this case that I don't?" Cerova asked Wilson once Washington was back inside.

"Possible serial killer. There was a similar death in California last week. We should have our file to you shortly," he answered concisely as he motioned toward the body. "As for the butterflies and the smell, see for yourself."

Officer Thompson did the honors, pulling back a corner of the sheet. "What the hell?" Cerova muttered in disbelief at the strong floral scent that exuded from the blanket of butterflies covering the body.

"We've caught several already and I weighed down the sheet to trap in as many as possible until the techs gets here. Plus, it was freaking everyone out." Thompson explained as he gingerly secured the corner.

"Good thinking," she responded. "The press would have a field day if they caught sight of this and that's the last thing I need this morning." Cerova had the gnawing feeling that it was going to be one of those cases: a strange one that goes nowhere and is never explained.

"I need coffee," she declared.

"I'm sure Willy could brew up a fresh pot for us," Wilson suggested.

"And give you a chance to interview the other potential witnesses?" she filled in the blanks.

"Just because you normally find me lurking in morgues doesn't mean I don't know *how* to do field work," he countered as he held the front door of the Hummingbird open for her. "My treat."

A wave of warmth greeted them. Neither had been to the dive before and the patrons of the Hummingbird were a mixed and motley bag. For more than a few of them, shabby would have been a generous descriptor. Uniforms were already taking statements.

"So you don't remember *anything*?" one officer incredulously asked the group of four youths who were barely holding themselves together under the sudden and unexpected police presence. The eldest among them spoke for the group, knuckles white against the table. "No sir, I'm sorry." The others nodded mutely. Their pupils were so dilated, they looked as if they were smuggling shark eyes. *Worse trip ever*, Wilson thought as he gestured for two cups of coffee. The cook was already on the same page and the coffee machine was hissing as it brewed another pot. Everyone inside could use a strong cup of joe.

It was the same refrain throughout the Hummingbird—no one remembered anything, and some were not fairing as well as the kids. Cerova immediately ordered the kitchen closed, which regretfully included the coffee. They were going to have to test all the food and drinks to see if everyone had been drugged. The uniforms started letting people leave once they had their personal and contact information, and Cerova turned her attention toward Jake Beals.

The TV detective was sitting alone at the counter. She pulled herself together before addressing the actor; Murphy was one of her favorite characters on the show. As Cerova introduced herself, Wilson stayed back, deferring to her lead.

"Thank you for staying, Mr. Beals. Do you remember anything?" she left the question wide open.

"Not really, but I think I got punched," he said, running his hand against the tender left side of his jaw.

"It is odd to land on one side of the jaw in a fall," she concurred. "We can have the medics check you out before you leave. Do you remember getting into a fight?"

He shook his head.

"Is this where you were sitting while you ate?" she motioned to the counter.

He hesitated. "I think so. At least, my coat was here and this is my normal order."

She noted the second plate, coffee cup, and used utensils next to his. "Who were you with?"

Beals looked at the counter and cocked his head. "I wasn't with anyone." Unlike the previous statement, he said it with utter certainty, which caught Wilson's attention.

The door chime rang as Detective Marshall Collins came in from the cold. He lived in the suburbs and it took him a little longer to get into the city for early morning calls. Not that he was worried. He knew his partner would have everything well in hand. Collins knew he was only ever going to be a detective, but Cerova was going to go a lot farther.

"Sorry I'm late, Jenn. Traffic was a bear, but I brought coffee," he spoke immediately. With over twenty years of experience in homicide, he was significantly older than her, but they had cobbled together something of a system in their three years as partners. There was little she couldn't forgive if you brought her coffee.

"Collins, you're an angel," she declared as she took the warm cup from him. There was an awkward moment when it suddenly dawned on her that her partner and fictional Detective Murphy were of a similar build and wearing a variation of the same tired suit. "Mr. Beals, this is my partner, Detective Collins. Collins, this is Jake Beals of *Cold Blue: Detroit*. We were just trying to ascertain who he was dining with this morning."

"Wait, if he's your partner, then who's that?" the actor pointed to Wilson.

"He's a fed," Collins answered. "You think Detroit PD pays us enough to afford a suit like that?"

Before Beals could question why federal agents were involved, Washington spoke up from behind the counter. "Jake, you were with arthritis girl."

Beals's face was a complete blank. "Who?"

"Young blonde, real looker. You said she was the corpse," Washington tried to jog his memory.

"The corpse?" the actor repeated.

"From the show. Man, your noodle really is scrambled," Washington remarked before speaking slowly as one did to a child. "You came in after your morning gig with the show's latest dead body, who happened to be one fine-ass young lady. Sweet thing but a little slow on the uptake, which is probably why you brought her here."

Beals threw up his hands. "Sounds like my type but I honestly don't remember. Sorry."

Cerova notched her head for visual confirmation that the rumble she heard outside was in fact the CSI van. *What took them so long?* She was anxious to get the unusual body packed up before rush hour traffic started in earnest.

"Thank you for your time, Mr. Beals. Officer Thompson will take your information and the name of someone at the production company who can help us track down your breakfast companion. Then you're free to go."

She and Collins headed out the door but Wilson stayed behind and jotted down the details for himself.

Chapter Ten

Battle Creek, Michigan, USA
9th of March, 8:25 a.m. (GMT-5)

Megan Anderson carefully wiped away the last of her tears but it was no good. Her eyes were bloodshot and swollen, even if they were temporarily dry. She rummaged through her bag for a pair of sunglasses; the aviators obscured her eyes nicely. Then she pulled her hair up and tucked it into a hat. The fewer identifying physical characteristics she had, the better.

It wasn't much of a plan, but she knew she had to keep moving and get off the grid as soon as possible. It was only a matter of time before the police started looking for her. She'd watched enough TV to know that the cops could trace a person's phone, credit cards, and even their rental car via GPS. She had grabbed everything from her hotel and pulled out her daily withdrawal limit on the ATM before leaving Detroit. Instead of returning the rental car at the airport, she had driven it to the closest branch in her hometown.

She waited until the rental agency's sign switched from "closed" to "open" before requesting a ride-share to take her to her parents' home. Once she had the driver's ETA, she grabbed her bags and handed over the keys to the lone employee manning the counter.

Although technically within the city limits, the family home was still a farm even though all the agrarian activity was leased out on an annual basis to a different family. As soon as she arrived and settled with the driver, she switched off her mobile. In the movies, they couldn't trace it if it wasn't on. She hoped that part was more fact than fiction because anywhere she could get a prepaid phone wasn't open yet.

She went straight for the outbuildings, bypassing the house altogether. Both her parents should be at work—her dad either at the office or on a call, and her mom on the breakfast shift—but she didn't want to risk running into them. If she saw them, the tears would just start all over again. Then she would have to explain what happened and all she wanted to do was forget.

She pushed back the wave of emotion that threatened to crash down over her and stuck to the plan. Her car—her dad's old VW Beetle—was parked in one of the barns. He always kept it tuned up and road ready so she'd have something to drive whenever she was home. She'd eventually have to ditch it, but for now, it was the superior choice over a rental car. There was no computer chips in it to track.

But the car wasn't the only thing stashed in the barn for safekeeping. Inside one of the unused horse stalls was a massive old safe hidden behind a few bales of hay. There, her dad kept cash, gold, and silver coins; he bought the safe after the economic crash nearly wiped them out. She carefully set the bales aside and turned the thick dial, keying in the combination—a collection of important family dates. She loaded her bag with stacks of cash, uncertain how much money she'd need, but left the gold and silver.

She briefly considered leaving a note, letting them know she was okay and that she would explain everything later. Her dad regularly checked on the safe every few weeks, but she knew he would come sooner if he noticed the car was gone or the police paid them a visit. She had no doubt her parents would cover for her, but where would that leave them? She dismissed the idea of a note—that way, they could honestly tell the police they hadn't heard from her.

Her wide eyes fell on the loaded gun next to the stack of coins. Part of her thought it would be a good idea to have some protection, especially if she was going to be carrying around all that cash. Then her dad's voice echoed in her head: *Never point a gun at anything you aren't planning to shoot.* Anderson closed the safe and spun the dial with the firearm still inside. She didn't want to hurt anyone else.

She turned the key in the Bug's ignition. The sound of the sputtering engine as it warmed up reminded her of happier times, when she'd finally made friends in high school and they'd tool around town in her crazy ancient hippy ride. When the biggest worry was who liked who and what they were going to wear to prom. The future seemed so big and promising. Now, she was hiding from the law.

As she engaged the clutch, she realized she'd reached the end of her pre-thought-out plans. She had cash and a car, but no real destination. The obvious choice was to cross the border into Canada, but once she went on that path, there was no going back. She would be walking away from her budding acting career, her parents, her friends—everything that mattered.

There had to be a way out of this. After all, it was self-defense on both counts. They attacked her, and she didn't mean to hurt them. She had just wanted to get away. Had things happened any other way, she would have gone straight to the police and called her parents. But who would believe a rainbow had shot out of her hand? That her attackers fell over and melted like a candle left in a hot car? Even if they didn't put her in prison, they'd put her in the loony bin for sure.

After the first time, she kept looking over her shoulder and waited for someone to show up at her landlady's place. She had images of Mrs. Johnson on the evening news playing in her head. "She was such a nice girl. Quiet, clean, never caused any problems."

When no one came after a few days and she got the part on *Cold Blue: Detroit*, it was easy to focus on the future and mentally sequester the whole incident as a bad fever dream. There were no witnesses, so who was to say what happened? No one could place her there, and the more times she told herself that nothing had happened, the more she believed it.

But Darren was different. They had history and there were plenty of witnesses who saw him throw the punch that downed Jake before grabbing her and pulling her outside. If only that was all they saw. She couldn't pretend it didn't happen and her brain kept replaying those final moments. She was tired. So tired.

Hands on the wheel, she steadied herself. "Only a few more hours to go," she promised her reflection in the rearview mirror. "Then you can sleep." She shifted into first gear and released the clutch, driving away in the cold morning air. The vapor trail of warm exhaust immediately dissipated behind her. Soon, it was like she had never been there at all.

When things started to open, she stopped for some food. Blueberry pancakes seemed like another life ago. She paid cash and couldn't imagine how people operated before debit cards and smart phones. Handling change alone was maddening—where did one keep all those coins? As she sat down with her small sandwich and baked chips, she unconsciously reached for her phone before remembering why it was turned off. She couldn't recall the last time she'd gone hours without checking in to see what was up. She ran her fingers over the blank black screen and it felt comforting, even through there was nothing to tap or swipe.

She resolved to pick up a prepaid phone after she finished eating but realized having a phone was only half of it. Sure, she could keep an eye on the news, but all her contacts and apps would be linked to a dead phone. She didn't have anyone's number memorized, even if she wanted to call for help. At very least, she needed to write down all the important phone numbers. Her thumb hovered above the on button. *Better earlier than later*, she convinced herself and pulled out a notepad and pen as the familiar icon lit up the screen.

*****

Once Wilson got a hold of *Cold Blue: Detroit's* assistant director, he had a name: Megan Jillian Anderson. He left the set with her phone number and the name of her hotel. Unfortunately, she wasn't answering her phone and she wasn't in her room. When he helped himself inside to check, he found it hastily cleared out even though she was still checked in.

Meanwhile, the analysts made quick work pulling together background information. Wilson skimmed through the file in his fifth-floor office until something caught his eye: her current address was listed in LA in one of the neighborhoods abutting the Kenneth Hahn State Recreational Area. Never one to believe in coincidence, he took a closer look.

Megan Jillian Anderson, twenty-four years old, daughter of Mr. James Anderson (plumber) and Mrs. Elisha Anderson (restaurant greeter) of Battle Creek, Michigan. Attended four years at the University of Michigan, Ann Arbor with double undergraduate degrees in business and performing arts. After college, Anderson moved to LA and started her acting career—extra work, a few commercials, and some bit-speaking parts. No current employment other than her acting gigs.

Wilson shrugged. *Promising start but probably not enough to pay her bills. Are her parents footing the bills or is she moonlighting off the books?* He picked up the head shot he'd gotten from the assistant director—she was certainly attractive enough to do elite-level escort service. He put in a request for the analysts to comb the LA local escort sites for a matching picture.

She was not a registered magician and her background was thin on the legal front. She had two speeding tickets and an expired restraining order that she'd extended three times—for six months each time—during her university days. The order was against an ex-boyfriend named Darren Ward. Wilson sent another request to the Mine for information regarding Ward; litigant histories weren't included in the vanilla background check.

He'd just clicked in the request when the analysts sent him an alert that Anderson had pulled out her maximum daily limit at the ATM two blocks away from her hotel at 5:45 am and returned her rental car at the Battle Creek location fifty-five minutes ago. The last ping off a cell tower was near there, but that was over forty-five minutes ago. *Smart kid doing a runner in her home turf,* Wilson surmised.

He had them track her phone activity since last night, including incoming numbers. A couple of hundred dollars wasn't going to go far and if she was in trouble, she'd likely reach out to friends and family. He geared up and changed his status to out of office to make sure he got any additional information the analysts uncovered before leaving for Battle Creek.

He wasn't sure how she fit into the butterfly killings, but he knew he had to get to her before Detroit PD did. If she wasn't dangerous, it was dangerous to be around her. He had nothing in common with a twenty-four-year-old actress, but he was going to have to start thinking like one.

Just as he was passing Jackson, he got another message from the Mine: Anderson's phone had just pinged in Rosebush, MI. No incoming or outgoing calls were made and it was no longer transmitting. Wilson pulled onto the shoulder and turned on his hazards. *Where the hell is Rosebush?* He pulled up the map and got his answer: a little town in the middle of nowhere.

He revisited Anderson's file and the information the analysts had sent him in subsequent requests. He was looking for hints of where she could be heading because Rosebush was definitely not the fastest route to the Canadian border. An expanded property search uncovered a house northwest of Houghton Lake, owned by Anderson's mother by way of her late father. It wasn't listed as a primary or secondary residence, and according to their taxes, they rented it out during deer hunting season.

Wilson grunted. *Great, another hunting lodge,* he sarcastically thought as he put in a request for satellite images.

Michigan was a far cry from the Yorkshire moors and all signs pointed to fae rather than fiends, but that didn't stop his limbic system from replaying his encounter with the six-armed claws of the amorphous demon named Pretakhuni summoned by the late Shyam Bhatt, PhD. By all accounts, he should have died in the damp heather but for his new augmenter abilities and the power of a magical ring called Andvaranaut.

He crammed the memory and the feelings down. This was the best lead he had. He plugged the address into his GPS and it rerouted him north.

Chapter Eleven

Houghton Lake, Michigan, USA
9th of March, 2:20 p.m. (GMT-5)

According to the satellite images of the area, a long dirt road was the only access onto the Andersons' property. The house proper was off the road by several hundred yards, nestled in a small clearing surrounded by woods—an ideal setup for deer hunting. The only other structure was a small, freestanding garage built several decades after the house.

Wilson was checking the images against his phone's directions when the gas pump's automatic shut-off clicked. He put the nozzle back into its cradle and closed up his gas tank. He wasn't far now but the drizzle made the last ten miles slow and tedious—just enough to make the roads slick and difficult to see.

It was loosely graveled but that changed when he turned off the main road. The path was slippery and he avoided driving in the tire tracks that had recently slogged through the mud. Someone had driven there recently and he shut off his app once there were no more turns to take. Whatever concentration wasn't needed to keep the car on the road was spent esoterically scanning the magical influences. *Think, think, think…* He was not going to be caught unaware at *this* hunting house.

The dirt road dead-ended into the Andersons' lot, and the property finally came into view. The house was a small, two-story clapboard painted white with green trim. The broad porch had rocking chairs and small tables spread from end to end. There were no vehicles parked in plain sight, but Wilson traced the tire marks into the closed garage.

He pulled his car onto the gravel patch to the side of the house and observed. There was nothing obviously magical so far, nor was there movement in any of the windows. He cut off his engine and listened. There was no one calling from the house or any dogs barking. He couldn't even hear the traffic on the distant country road this far off.

He silently exited the 911 and climbed up the front-porch stairs. His probing will found no magical wards and protections. Were the circumstances different, he would have knocked on the door as FBI, but as it looked like Anderson was on the run, he opted for infiltration. He knew someone had been there, and it was just a matter of if they were *still* inside.

The lock on the front door was nothing special and he had it open in no time. The quiet persisted inside; even the hinges swiveled without noise. The entry opened into the living room with a flight of stairs leading up to the second floor. While most of the furniture was covered by white bedsheets, the dust cover over the worn-but-homey couch had been removed and the pillows rearranged all onto one side. He closed the front door and with Glock in hand, crossed the aged pine floor. He put his hand against the cushions: they were still warm to the touch. Someone was home and hiding.

As he went from room to room on the ground floor, he couldn't help but elicit a few squeaks from the old floor. Each one seemed terribly loud to him, but nothing stirred. When he was satisfied the first floor was empty, he faced the stairs. In his experience, stairs, particularly old wooden ones, were the noisiest part of a house.

He'd made it halfway up in stealth when a loose floorboard gave him away. Megan Anderson appeared at the top of the stairs, baseball bat in hand. She looked fierce until she saw the gun in Wilson's hand. *I should have brought the gun!* she chided herself as she yelped and ran for the master bedroom, one of the few rooms in the house with a lock.

She managed to shut the door behind her but Wilson came up with incredible speed and rammed his shoulder against it, popping it open before she had a chance to lock it. She screamed and like a cornered animal, she stepped back and raised her hands against his charge. A prism of light shot out of her palm toward the doorway.

Anderson expected him to cry out as he melted like the others. When she heard no such commotion, she looked up and saw her assailant was no longer there. Instead, there was just a blur and before she could react, she suddenly felt very sleepy. Her body collapsed as she lost consciousness, and Wilson, augmented just beyond human speed, caught her in mid-fall.

He placed her on the bed and got to work. His knockout spell should reliably buy him twenty to thirty minutes but he wanted her secured before he did any investigation. He brought up a wooden chair from the kitchen and the dust cover from the couch. With swift decisive movements, he sliced the cloth into strips with the small but razor-sharp knife he always carried.

He placed Anderson's still-limp form on the chair and tied her extremities to it. It wouldn't stop a practitioner from using magic but it would make it more difficult. She'd raised her hand right before the spell went off, and only advanced practitioners could wield magic without the typical somatics that accompanied the exertion of will.

Then, he checked the back of her neck for an acquisitionist's mark. Once he was certain there was none, he wrapped another strip of cloth over her eyes and stripped one of the pillows, putting its case over her head. Magic was hard to target without sight for those who were used to relying on vision. It was just another precaution, but Wilson wasn't taking any chances until he knew more.

With Anderson secure, he finally started his investigation. He blew salt from his caster where she'd cast her spell and the white grains immediately started moving. When the pattern settled into the same one he'd seen in LA, he snapped a picture before breaking the magical signature with his foot.

If it were just the deaths in LA and Detroit, he would have considered putting a bullet in her, taking care of the body, and then calling it a day, but there were too many things that didn't make sense. Why did her magical signature look fae? If she could practice magic, why appear at the top of the stairs with a baseball bat? If she was a cold-blooded killer, why did she turn her face away when the light shot out of her hand?

Of course, there was always the option that Megan Anderson wasn't as she seemed. He pulled out his keys and flipped through the ring until he came to a slim bar of cold iron not much bigger than a matchstick. Cold iron was forged at a lower temperature than normal iron via the use of magic, and it was anathema to faeries. If Anderson was fae in disguise—for example, a changeling—it would burn at the slightest touch.

He readied his will in case the pain woke her from his spell prematurely and pressed the tip against the inside of Anderson's forearm just above her bound wrists. There was no reaction. He tried pressing the length of the bar against other parts of her body to make sure it wasn't a false negative but Anderson didn't show the slightest bit of discomfort.

"Huh," Wilson uttered, baffled. He'd mostly convinced himself that was what it was going to be. He put away the cold iron and sent what he had to the Mine to see if Chloe and Dot had any theories why a human practitioner would have such a fae-looking signature. After a few minutes, they responded that if she were a new practitioner that'd had interaction with the fae, either recently or in her youth before her power blossomed, her signature could possibly have a fae-ish predilection.

Wilson considered it a plausible explanation. That would account for her ungainly attack. It was so slow and crude that Wilson could have easily avoided it, even without being augmented. Perhaps that was the connection between the various butterfly murders—a practitioner coming into power under the influence of the fae, or perhaps a fae object? He took the opportunity to do a quick search of her possessions and the house but found nothing else magical.

Giving up, Wilson sat on the bed opposite Anderson waiting for her to rouse from his spell. When she came to, she immediately started to struggle against her ties but didn't scream. *She's a clever one*, he thought. Most people would have yelled for help if they found themselves in such circumstances. However, that would only give away the fact that she was awake to whoever had tied her up; if she has been left alone, she had a much better chance of breaking out and escaping if she stayed quiet.

"Ms. Anderson," Wilson broke the silence and she immediately froze. "I'm Special Agent Wilson of the FBI and I'm investigating two rather unusual deaths—one in Los Angeles a week ago and one in Detroit this morning."

She squared her shoulders defiantly and replied sharply. "Nice try. FBI don't break into people's houses and tie them up."

He allowed himself a small smile since she couldn't see him. "And most people don't shoot killer rainbows out of their hands, but here we are."

"It was self-defense…they attacked me," she said emphatically. "I didn't even know I could do that until last week!"

"I understand, but those two men are still dead and it won't take long for less understanding law enforcement to find you and start asking some very difficult questions," he laid the groundwork for negotiation. "If you promise to cooperate, I can take off the hood and you can tell me your side of the story."

"Can you untie me?" she pressed for more freedom.

"Not until I know how you fit into these deaths," he stated firmly. "But consider this. If my intent was to kill you, you would already be dead."

He let that sink in and she eventually answered, "Take off the hood." She was trying to sound tough but he could hear the slight tremor in her voice. She was terrified and putting on a brave face. He obliged and she breathed easier with her nose and mouth free of the pillowcase.

"You're going to feel me touch you but that's just so I can remove the blindfold. Don't make any sudden movements—the knife is very sharp," he warned her before carefully slicing through the fabric without severing even a single strand of her hair.

She blinked rapidly and desperately wanted to rub her eyes. They darted side to side as she got her bearings and was marginally relieved when she recognized the room. Then, she took a good look at Wilson. The man didn't match the voice; he'd sounded taller.

"Can I see some sort of identification?" she immediately requested. She wasn't even sure he was FBI, but if he was legit, he could be her ticket out of trouble.

"If it would make you feel better," Wilson answered drolly. He reached into his inner jacket pocket and held out his identification.

She ran her silvery eyes over the badge—the name and picture matched. Considering the mess she was in, that was better than nothing. She nodded and he returned the leather wallet to his pocket.

"You won't believe me," she challenged him.

"Try me," he offered as he took a seat.

She spoke plainly with clean and precise words, starting with the attack in the park in LA and ending with the Hummingbird. She was descriptive without any of the typical emotional color. It was one of the more refreshing interviews he'd sat through—no messy outbursts or appeals to deal with. Just the facts as she saw them. It felt like she was relaying a recipe rather than telling him how she'd accidentally killed two men with magic. Only she didn't know it was magic. She didn't know what it was, which was her stated reason for running away this morning.

When she finished, she asked a very simple question. "What are you going to do with me?"

That's a good question, he thought to himself as he examined her statement against what he already knew. She made no mention of butterflies in her account and she didn't appear to know that no one at the cafe could remember anything. It supported the theory that she was a new practitioner; even she didn't know what she was capable of. Either that, or she was a very good actress indeed. He looked her over again. On the whole, he believed her.

Wilson laid out her options. "The department that I work for is interested in neutralizing disruptive forces, not punishment. If you agree to cooperate with us further, we can help you find support for this newfound ability. This is entirely your choice and you can choose to handle it alone if that's what you want, but if you cannot control this power, I—or someone like me—will be sent to take care of the problem. Permanently."

Anderson weighed his carefully chosen words. "If I cooperate, can you get me out of this mess? I don't want to go to jail."

"That could be arranged," he affirmed.

That was all she needed to hear. "Done. Can you let me go now?"

Wilson pulled out his knife again and Anderson held her

questions and kept quiet, not wanting to derail her imminent freedom. "My apologies for the damage and treatment, but I had to make sure you couldn't hurt anyone else until I ascertained your role in the recent events," he said as he severed the fabric.

She rubbed her wrists and extended her legs before standing up and taking a few steps around the room. The door was closed and locked, and he watched her for signs of bolting but she made no such overtures. Despite their rocky start, it would appear Megan Anderson was going to play nice.

He readied himself for a litany of questions but wasn't expecting what came out of her mouth next. "There's someone coming up the drive. Are you expecting company? Because I'm not."

Wilson didn't hear a car but when he checked the window, there was indeed a nondescript black midsized vehicle poorly working its way up the muddy drive. He was trying to work out how she'd heard it when he hadn't when he saw four identical white men with perfect black hair exit the car. They were dressed in matching black suits.

The gears started turning in Wilson's head. *Shit, mantids.* He didn't have much time. "They aren't with me, but they mean trouble. Do you have a gun?"

"Do you think I would have come at you with a baseball bat if I'd had a gun?" she sarcastically answered his question with a question.

With a flip of the wrist, he passed her his knife, handle first. "Then take this. I'm going to meet them at the door and try to get them to leave quietly, but if I fail, stab at their faces. They hate that and it may drive them away."

His willingness to arm her right after he'd just had her tied up threw her off kilter and she realized just how much danger she was in. She took the knife and nodded seriously.

"Stay here and I'll come get you when the coast is clear," he instructed her before leaving the room. He heard the door close and lock behind him.

Chapter Twelve

Houghton Lake, Michigan, USA
9th of March, 3:10 p.m. (GMT-5)

Wilson changed his magazine to regular bullets as he came down the stairs. There was no point in using banishment bullets against the mantid hit squad; they were ultimately native to the mortal realm as they were originally extraterrestrial. A breeding population had taken up residence in the Magh Meall after several generations made it clear that the Earth was chockablock with hominids, which they regarded as uncouth hairless murder monkeys. There they became the favored hired help of the fae. They were their enforcement arm in the mortal realm, sent out to break knees and bash heads to ensure a desirable resolution in rare cases where fae magic was proving ineffectual.

As their name implied, mantid physiology resembled praying mantises, only human-sized. Their mouthparts allowed for verbal communication and the maneuverable spines at the end of their spiky forelegs allowed them relatively complex tool use. They were a predatory species that had become adept at magical camouflage during their stay in the Magh Meall, assuming the forms of other creatures via their glamours. Over the millennia of employment by the fae, mantids had developed an understanding of humans that eluded their employers, who were only interested in humans as slaves—the kernel of truth buried in so many fairytales of stealing children and tricking people into the middle lands and eventually Fae itself, from which they would never return.

The mantids' only real weakness was their visual spectrum. It skewed strongly toward the ultraviolet, and when they pretended to be human, nearly all the detail they used to distinguish one mantid from the other was lost to the visual spectrum of humans. Consequently, while they appeared unique to each other, their glamours often looked identical to humans. It was one of the hallmark clues one was dealing with mantids. That was what tipped off Wilson immediately—it was highly unlikely a set of quadruplets entered government service, worked in the same unit, and wore the same clothes.

Wilson watched through the small curtained window as they approached. Once they reached the porch, he opened the front door with a wide smile, keeping his right hand inconspicuously close to his Glock. "Good afternoon, gentlemen. What can I do for you?" he asked with a folksy twang.

The mantids exchanged looks but didn't speak. Instead, they communicated with each other through scent, something they did when they didn't want to be overheard. Wilson could faintly pick up the odor of crushed ants, the only part of their olfactory communication that humans could perceive with their limited sense of smell.

The leader of the squad stepped forward and spoke. "Yes, good citizen, we are from the government. We are seeking Megan Jillian Anderson for an interview at the station," it replied stiffly. They did a good impression of looking human, but they didn't have the finer things down. Their speech and mannerisms were close but still off. It was like listening to a foreigner speak your native tongue—even when they got everything technically right, you could still tell they weren't from around here.

"Of course, anything for the government! Please come in and take a seat. I'll call her cell and tell her you need to see her," Wilson responded gregariously. He wanted them inside and with a reason to remain nonviolent, at least long enough to get some information out of them before killing them.

More odors were exchanged. "She is not here?"

"Sorry, no. She just stepped out a few minutes ago. Not sure where she went, but she should come back once I let her know someone from the government wants to talk to her. Otherwise it may be hours before she returns," Wilson continued his yarn. They shuffled past him and took a seat on the couch. "Please excuse the mess. I was just in the middle of doing some spring cleaning." They nodded their heads vigorously in agreement—yes, the cleaning we *all* do in spring!

He closed the front door and walked into the kitchen, popping his head out into the living room to politely ask,

"Would you like anything to drink while you wait?"

"No. That is not required," said the lead mantid.

"As you wish," Wilson replied innocently. He gathered his will and wrapped it around himself as Liu had taught him to do. Once he felt the surge of his augmentation, he stepped out of the kitchen, Glock in hand and pointed at the head of the leader. He didn't like putting the mantid between him and the stairs that led to Anderson, but this was the only place where he could maintain a good ten feet between himself and them. Getting close with a gun was a poor decision when dealing with humans and utterly foolish against the mantids' significantly quicker reflexes.

"Ms. Anderson is under the protection of the Salt Mine. Your orders are counter to my orders," he said flatly. Wilson couldn't tell if invoking the Salt Mine had an effect; he was not well versed in the meaning of insect expression and posture. However, the crushed ant smell intensified as they looked back and forth amongst themselves.

They moved with such precision, traveling the same speed throughout the duration of a movement and stopping exactly on target without over or under compensation. By comparison, human movement was mushy and messy. It was unnerving to watch them too closely but Wilson didn't flinch.

"That is an unexpected difficulty," the lead mantid answered. "Certainly there is room for negotiation."

Wilson opened his mouth to speak but only got out

"There—" before the mantid closest to him exploded from its seat, arms outstretched and spikes ready. Even with his augmented speed, he barely had time to double tap it in the head.

Then he finished his sentence as if nothing had happened, "—isn't room to negotiate." As the body on the floor leaked green liquid, the glamour wore off and the full insectoid underneath was revealed. "There are three of you left, and I only need one of you to answer my questions. It's entirely up to you how many in your squad walk out of here alive."

Morale quickly broke with one of theirs dead on the floor. Humans were not known for being so fast. There was a congress of odors that went well beyond Wilson's nose. Eventually, the leader said, "Speak."

Without lowering his gun, he asked, "Who hired you?"

"We were hired by the fae," it answered.

"Which fae?"

Again the crushed ant smell swelled in what Wilson could only image was a spirited argument. After a moment the leader responded, "House Tantali." Wilson recognized the name as one of the lesser fae houses.

"And the mission? What has Ms. Anderson done to annoy House Tantali?" he pressed.

The delay this time was longer and Wilson wasn't sure if the smell increased as he was starting to go nose deaf to the scent. When the answer finally came, it confirmed what he had suspected as soon as he saw them pull up. "We do not know her insult, but our mission was her death." Wilson tried to gauge the truth of the words, but gave up—they were simply too alien.

"Like the fae, I am true to my word. Since you have been so cooperative, you're free to go. Slowly," he added as a caveat. "One at a time starting with you." He nodded to the mantid closest to the door. "Once he's in the car, the next can go."

The mantids shuffled out one by one until it was just the squad leader and Wilson left in the living room. "Don't come back," he warned it. "Don't try to make good on your deal with the Tantali. Refund their payment, mourn your dead, and walk away. If you persist, the Salt Mine will hunt down your hive in the Magh Meall and dig it out of the ground forever. *We* protect ours and we have jurisdiction here, not House Tantali nor any of the fae."

The leader remained silent as he backed out of the house and into the car. The engine was already going and the vehicle pulled out as soon as he was inside. Just as it turned off the property, he heard Anderson's footsteps on the landing. "You can come down," he hollered. "They're gone."

She descended, knife still in hand. "I know you told me to stay inside the room until you gave the all clear, but I heard gunshots and got worried." When she turned the corner, the sight of the mantid corpse on the circular rug caused her to gasp and drop the knife.

"Don't worry, it will disappear on its own in a few hours," he reassured her as he holstered his gun. Mantids had a complex biochemistry, and their corpses decomposed quickly. In a matter of hours, there would only be a little dust left—nothing a quick vacuuming or good beating couldn't take care of. He picked up the knife, folded it, and returned it to his pocket.

"Let's go into the kitchen and leave it be," he suggested calmly, guiding her with a gentle hand. Anderson let herself be led and dumbly took a seat at the table. Wilson started opening cabinets until he found a kettle and a selection of tea and some instant coffee. He let the faucet run until the water ran clear and put the full kettle on the burner. "Tea or coffee?"

"I don't like hot tea," she answered vacantly.

"Coffee it is then," he responded before quietly starting work on the beverages, giving her time to privately come to terms with the dead mantid in her living room. He pulled out two mugs from the cabinet and gave them a good wipe before spooning in the powdered coffee. When the kettle whistled, he stirred while he poured, reconstituting the freeze-dried crystals. He put the sugar on the table and checked the fridge for milk but found it completely empty except for two open boxes of baking soda. He sat down opposite her and waited. In his experience, people would start to ask questions when they were ready for answers. To say anything before that was just wasting breath.

"What the hell is going on?!" she exclaimed when she could

finally put words to what was churning in her head.

"You are caught up in something bigger than yourself. That guy that attacked you in LA? He wasn't himself. He was compelled by a faerie. And those goons? They were sent to kill you by another group of fae," Wilson answered plainly. She'd handled everything else so well that he didn't feel the need to sugarcoat things.

"Fairies? Like fairytales and Disney?" she said, trying to wrap her brain around the concept.

He equivocally bobbed his head. "Sort of. Faeries are real and very dangerous. They're nothing like Tinkerbell or fairy godmothers."

"What do they want with me?" she asked.

"I don't know, but I aim to find out," he responded. Much to her surprise, she believed him. *Is this how Stockholm Syndrome works*? she wondered but kept it to herself.

"Does the name Tantali mean anything to you?" he asked. Anderson shook her head and sipped her coffee. "What about Dökkálfar?"

"No, but it sounds like it should be an alien race in Star Trek," she commented.

Wilson reviewed her story. "In LA, did that guy say anything to you when he came out from behind the stand?"

"I don't think so," she said weakly.

"Please, try to remember. I hate to press, but it could give me some clue as to what is going on," he said candidly.

Anderson took a deep breath and closed her eyes, replaying the scene in her mind's eye. She'd been jogging and listening to music. It was just starting to get dark but there was still some light. And then he grabbed her from behind. Her heart raced and breath quickened at the memory. She pushed past the fear—she wasn't there anymore. She was safe in the kitchen with a cup of coffee. He was screaming at her, calling her a bitch. He wanted something. What was it?

"My hair," she said. She touched her honey blonde tresses and opened her eyes. "He was pulling on my hair."

Wilson's eyebrow raised. "Are you sure?"

"Yes," she affirmed with certainty. "He said, 'I need your hair, bitch.' Does that help?"

Chapter Thirteen

Detroit, Michigan, USA
9th of March, 7:40 p.m. (GMT-5)

It hadn't taken much convincing for Anderson to go with Wilson, even though she initially wanted to drive herself. However, she got into the 911 with her things once he pointed out that driving a car registered to either her or in her dad's name was a bad idea. The long drive from Houghton Lake to Detroit provided hours of question and answer time. Wilson explained the basics to her. Magic was real. Some people could do it, but not everyone, and there were lots of different types; being able to do one type didn't mean you could do another. His most important message was that she needed to get her magic under control before she hurt someone else or herself.

He explained karmic cost and the bad luck that was coming her way with two deaths by magic at her hands. She rebutted that she had good luck after the first death—she'd landed the *Cold Blue: Detroit* role. However, she conceded the point when Wilson replied, "The role that got you back into Michigan where you just happened to run into your stalker ex-boyfriend *and* ended up on the run from the police—that good luck?"

Karma wasn't always direct in its approach.

She was a quick study, often repeating what he'd said verbatim when asked to demonstrate understanding. For someone whose life was recently turned upside down, she was taking it remarkably in stride. Once she had the broad strokes, he probed a little deeper into the fae angle, seeing if she had any memories of accidentally entering the Magh Meall, being visited by fae, or being gifted something supernatural, but nothing came of it. Even though the conversation was light, he was still on guard, pinning down her mannerisms, speech patterns, and physical ticks. It was something he did whenever he could as he never knew when that information would come in handy.

Normally, he would have left a new practitioner in distress with Herman Aloysius Hardwick, the owner of the nightclub 18 is 9. Despite his personal dislike of the man, he was reliable in his passion for taking in strays who needed help. Hardwick had several spare rooms on the top floor of the bar and personal security onsite as well as magical security capable of dealing with basic threats.

But this was different. Wilson felt sure that she'd be safe from that particular mantid clan, but there were always others. Anderson was too hot to drop off at 18 is 9—it would put everyone there at risk. Mantids wouldn't hesitate to kill everyone in the bar if they thought that was what was required to accomplish their mission. There was something uniquely special about her if the Dökkálfar wanted some of her hair and the Tantali wanted her dead.

While it wasn't his first choice, he decided the best practical option was for her to stay with him at the safest residence in Detroit, his sanctum sanctorum, the 500. Once she was settled for the night, he could summon up information using a sample of her hair. Ideally, that would reveal something useful and get her out of the 500 as quickly as possible.

The conversation had died down by the time Wilson drove down West Lafayette and the four stories of the 500 came into view. He pulled up to the massive steel slab that functioned as a garage door.

"Big place," Anderson said, pushing forward in her seat to look upward.

"It's smaller on the inside," Wilson explained, pressing the control that kicked in the hydraulics. The moving slab revealed the emptiness of the three-story garage behind. He exercised his will and lowered the ward against magicians so that Anderson wouldn't trigger it. The engine purred under his facile hands as he released the break and tapped on the accelerator, but just as soon as it started, the car abruptly came to a stop—like hitting an invisible wall. Inside Wilson's head, multiple alarms went off and without thinking about it, he launched his will like a bludgeon against Anderson, knocking her out cold.

Shit. He extended his will and silenced the three alarms in his head, noting their context as he went: the one that prevented magical tracers, one that hedged out ghosts, and one that kept the 500 untouchable to fae. He reversed the car, parked along the curb, and double-clicked the button for the door, returning it to its down position. He pulled out his phone and sent a text message to the Mine: *Coming in hot. 5 minutes. Living package included. Need immediate processing.*

It wasn't until he put the phone away that he noticed a familiar smell inside the car: the same floral that had lingered over the corpses. He looked over at the unconscious form of Anderson in the passenger's seat. *What the hell are you?*

It was a short drive to Zug Island from his place, made faster by the light traffic at this hour and his desire for answers. He gained entrance onto the island using David Watson's ID and magicked away any memory the gate guard might have had of him or the attractive unconscious blonde in his passenger seat. Instead of pulling into the covered parking garage as usual, he drove straight for the freight entrance.

Sometime prior to the CIA's purchase of the Salt Mine in the 1950s, Discretion Minerals had installed a deep freight elevator to facilitate moving heavy machinery. Prior to that, everything had to be disassembled, taken down in the smaller personnel elevator, and reassembled below. Although larger, the freight elevator still wasn't huge by modern standards. It was only suitable for a medium-sized box truck and no more than twenty tons of weight. But it was large enough for the Salt Mine's need.

On the rare occasions that agents needed to bring in something unknown, dangerous, or both, the freight entrance was used instead of the standard entrance to avoid the populated areas of the mine. The freight elevator led into a magical quarantine zone Leader had designed for such contingencies and the security procedures were adjusted accordingly.

The second Wilson had sent his text, it set into motion a cascade of activity as the well-oiled machine was fired up. Power was returned to the freight elevator and the upper levels of that part of the Mine, armed guards were called to duty, and an immediate donation was made on behalf of the incoming agent to cover any karmic cost incurred in the field. If they were using the freight entrance, there were already enough complications—no need to invite bad karma.

Everyone was ready and waiting by the time Wilson pulled his 911 into the shadowy entrance. He cut the engine and stayed in the vehicle until the heavy security door closed behind him. Then he exited the car with his hands up and in plain sight. He knew full well there were automatic rifles pointed at him from the hidden armored hidey-holes built into the elevator's superstructure. He didn't want to give them a reason to shoot.

He walked slowly to the panel on the side of the elevator and put his palm and eye against two scanners. It pinged and the light flashed green once it positively confirmed his identity.

The unmistakable backlit form of David LaSalle appeared from a remarkably well hidden door. Even though Wilson knew of its existence and general location, LaSalle still seemed to appear out of nowhere every time. Before him was a lead-lined containment trolley for objects. LaSalle did a cursory sweep and when he was satisfied, he spun his will to the unseen security. "Security detail dismissed. As always, thank you for your service," his crisp tenor announced.

The four heavily armed guards clambered down the access pegs and marched through the hidden door, which silently closed behind them and again disappeared.

"What do we have?" LaSalle's asked.

Dim light flooded the floor of the elevator when Wilson opened the passenger door. "Megan Anderson, incapacitated. I initially thought she was a new practitioner but she triggered three alarms at the 500: tracking, ghost, and fae. I'd like you to process her because she is not what she appears to be." As he spoke, he loaded her luggage into the containment trolley.

Something pinged on LaSalle's radar at the mention of the 500 but he gave nothing away in his demeanor or his voice. He merely replied, "Certainly," and put his palm and eye on the reader. A panel presented itself and he pressed a few buttons. Only then did the elevator start its noisy and slow descent.

There were no buttons to select a designated floor; the platform simply lurched to a halt in the middle of the shaft when it came level with a metal hatch. Wilson got Anderson out of the car and arranged her on his shoulders in a fireman's carry as LaSalle unsealed the hatch with another set of palm and retinal scanners and keypad.

The long corridor beyond the door was sheathed in metal. Even if someone dug through the salt walls, they'd encounter a metal barricade. The gentle slope turned before coming to another door, this one a spinning seal like a submarine door. Past that was another long passage lined with secured doors. LaSalle led Wilson to a ready room in the middle of the hallway and waited behind him. As Wilson gently placed Anderson onto the prepared metal bed and strapped her in, he parked the trolley in a corner.

Once the last restraint clicked into place, Wilson didn't even have time to turn around before the weight of LaSalle's gathered will crashed down on him.

When he woke, he was lying on a bed similar to the one he'd placed Anderson on except his arms and legs were free. He looked around the room and saw LaSalle, resting in the corner silently tapping away on his tablet but there was no sign of Anderson. Wilson did a quick physical and mental check—everything seemed find except for one killer headache.

"Welcome back to the land of the free," LaSalle greeted him. Wilson sat up gingerly and LaSalle tossed him a bottle of water. Wilson caught it with one hand and downed half of it in one go.

"I know you had to process me but did you have to jump me?" Wilson grilled him.

"A precaution but you're good now," LaSalle curtly replied.

"I was good before," Wilson asserted.

"No, you weren't. You'd been charmed," he bluntly corrected him.

"No I wasn't," Wilson automatically replied and laughed, but he instantly regretted it. His head hurt like hell. Instead, he categorically denied the possibility of it. "Even if someone did get the jump on me with a charm—which they wouldn't—I've got fail-safes to break them. Hell, I've even got a dead-man's switch if someone tries to charm me when I'm sleeping or unconscious. I've fail-safes on the fail-safes!"

In true form, LaSalle stayed cool and simply stated an observation. "They were more 'fails' than 'safes' in this instance."

Wilson rubbed his temples and gave a dismissive, "Whatever."

LaSalle decided to use this as a teachable moment and gave Wilson his full attention. "Answer me one question: when was the last time you invited someone you had just met into the 500? I've been there once and that was just because you were in trouble."

Wilson was unaccustomed to his precautions failing and it made him sour. Security was his thing, but LaSalle had made an irrefutable point. *What the hell happened? Why did I think it was a good idea?*

When Wilson didn't answer, LaSalle returned to tapping away at his tablet. "If it makes you feel any better, the alarms at the 500 were probably what snapped you out of it long enough to call it in. It was intricate and subtle, like unpicking lace."

Wilson finished his water and conceded. "Fine, say you're right. How'd she do it?"

"Don't know yet. I put her under and in isolation because taking care of you was the priority," he answered honestly. Agents were hard to replace and it was easier to fix one than find a new one.

"Could have been a bit gentler taking me out," Wilson grumbled. The longer he was awake, the more he suspected that not all of his headache was from the process.

"I wasn't sure how affected you were. I didn't want to miss," LaSalle explained and added to himself, *and you're stronger than you know now.*

Wilson gently nodded. He would have done the same thing—keep the charmed person engaged with the focus of their charm and attack from behind when the opportunity presented itself. He couldn't find fault with LaSalle securing one risk before dealing with the second, even if he happened to be on the receiving end of this particular divide and conquer technique.

"If you think you're okay, I'm going to start on her," LaSalle said, closing his tablet and standing up. He was a block of muscle, nearly a foot taller than Wilson and almost double his weight.

"Yeah, I'm fine. Can we wait here until the headache wears off?" Wilson asked.

"Sorry, can't," LaSalle answered curtly. "I expect it will take a while and I'm already behind schedule."

Wilson grimaced as he got off the bed. The pair made their way back to the elevator and up to the surface. Once on top, he opened the door to his car and gave LaSalle some parting information. "One thing—I've encountered a strange floral smell several times during this case and I smelled it again when I knocked Anderson out in my car. The pathologists believe it is butterfly sex pheromones, but I'm not sure that's all it is. I'm going to track it down in the library but I thought you should know before spending a lot of time in the same room with her."

"Thanks for the heads up. I'll take precautions," LaSalle said politely.

"And thanks for helping me out," Wilson reluctantly added.

LaSalle paused at the begrudging gesture. "Lots of water and get some food," he instructed Wilson.

He pulled the Porsche out of the freight elevator and circled back to the garage, parking it in his regular spot. There would be food in the cafeteria, and if nothing else, he had water and power bars in his office. He still had work to do tonight.

Chapter Fourteen

Detroit, Michigan, USA
9th of March, 9:00 p.m. (GMT-5)

Tonight was Salisbury steak night, and Wilson had a generous helping of mashed potatoes with it to help sop up all the gravy. Even though it was late, he helped himself to two cups of coffee. Not only would it help him in the forthcoming long night, it had the added benefit of working on his headache, which was down to a dull tension between the eyes.

While he chewed on dinner, he replayed his interactions with Anderson earlier in the day, trying to figure out when and how she'd gotten to him. Was it during the long drive back to Detroit? In the kitchen after the mantids had left? Or had it started earlier than that? Wilson thought his guard had been up the whole time and he found the fact that he couldn't nail down a turning point disconcerting.

He shrugged, bused his dishes, and left the cafeteria for his fifth floor office. LaSalle would suss it out of her and he'd have answers soon enough. Once he knew how she did it, he could tweak his defenses or build new ones to prevent it from happening again. In the meantime, he could investigate something that had been bothering him: the scent. There was a very special reference he wanted to access, but he'd need the librarians' help to get to it.

He picked up the brick that was the handle of his office phone and dialed down to the twins. It wasn't Bakelite, but it wasn't far off. While other aspects of the Mine's technology had changed with the times, Leader kept the ancient phone system around because it worked and it was impervious to any modern computer attacks. It also didn't hurt that it was cheaper to use what was already there.

Dot answered on the third ring. "What do you need? I'm busy." She knew full well it was Wilson thanks to the flashing lights on the phone console at the circular desk. It was as close as this phone system would get to caller ID.

Wilson was surprised to hear the surly sister answer; Chloe was the designated people person of the pair. He had expected to exchange a certain amount of social pleasantries before coming to the point. In the background, he heard Chloe's voice. "That's her way of saying 'Hello, Wilson, nice to hear from you again. What can we do for you?'"

He stifled a chuckle and got straight to the matter at hand, "I need access to *Liber Odores*." The encyclopedia of scents was a monumental work containing millions of specific odors—the world's oldest proverbial scratch and sniff book. The user could browse, picking scent after scent, and it would magically fill their nostrils with its essential aroma. In this way, it could expose people to odors they had never experienced before; the twins believed the book played a significant role in the development of perfumes wherever it traveled.

In addition, the book could also collect scents from the reader's memory, effectively creating a new entry in the encyclopedia. He didn't think he was dealing with a novel smell, but Wilson hoped to use this function to identify the elusive odor. *Liber Odores* would check the scent against all known to it, lest it create a duplicate entry—which would be unacceptable. In a way, it had the temperament of a lexicographer.

Dot didn't answer him right away. Instead, he heard the friction of her receiver rubbing against her clothes as she placed it against her chest and consulted her sister.

She returned to the line and informed him, "We'll come and get you," before brusquely hanging up. There were only a few people who had security clearance to access the sixth floor, and with LaSalle otherwise engaged, the twins had to collect him themselves.

He closed down his office and took a seat in one of the plush leather chairs in the lobby. He rose to meet them when he heard the noise of the elevator's approach. When the door opened, Chloe greeted him warmly and he and Dot exchanged nods.

The librarians were conjoined at the torso down to the hip, Chloe on the right and Dot on the left. They were broader than a single person, but not as wide as two. All their clothes had to be adapted to fit their unique physiology, and today, it was a shared checkerboard calf-length skirt with a sweater—it was a never ending battle against the constant 55°F temperature of the Mine.

Even if they were not literally joined at the hip, it was easy to tell they were sisters. They had the same nose, mouth, intelligent blue eyes, and thin blonde hair. They were both frighteningly smart with eidetic memories and shared a love of knowledge and order. That said, they were also very different and expressed their individuality in their hair, makeup, and accessories.

Chloe was preppy and cheerful with a colorful scarf around her neck, white on red polka dot cotton leggings, Mary Jane flats, and a pair of bronze dragonfly clips securing her coiffed blonde hair. Dot was goth and nihilistic with dark liner around her blue eyes and thin lips, thick black stockings with skulls woven in, and combat boots. Wilson wasn't sure he'd describe them as polar opposites, but he'd definitely say so if asked in their presence, if only to please them.

Chloe held up her palm and eye to the scanner and pressed the button for the sixth floor while Dot grilled him. "*Liber Odores*, eh? What's got you stumped?" They knew Wilson to be a cautious person by nature, and he wouldn't come within ten feet of that level of magic without good reason.

"Has to do with the butterfly deaths," he informed them. "A distinct odor at both crime scenes and then again in the car while I was bringing in the killer."

"So *you* were the urgent delivery," Chloe put two and two together. As the second line of defense, they had been notified the Mine was getting a package by freight per protocol. When the elevator stopped on the sixth floor, they proceeded to the stacks.

"Did anything come up when you were processed?" Dot inquired as they walked through the long saline halls lined with some of the rarest works on magic in the world.

"I got charmed," he said sheepishly.

That brought the twins to an abrupt halt. "What?" they exclaimed in unison. Chloe immediately asked what happened while Dot started to laugh. It was small at first but kept growing until it filled the air.

Chloe jabbed her sister in the side and gave him a sympathetic look. "It could happened to anyone," she delivered a platitude, but being a librarian, could not let a misstatement go uncorrected. "Obviously, not to Dot and I but to anyone else." As two minds in one body, they could not be charmed.

"Got charmed and had to be defragged, huh?" Dot teased as her laughter died off. He wasn't sure which was worse: Dot's derision or Chloe's patronizing kindness.

"LaSalle is looking into it, but what's important is that I'm good to go," he pressed on. It was safest to use the *Liber Odores* on the recently cleansed.

Dot was still chuckling as they took several turns that

ended in front of a standard security door. Chloe opened it with a palm and retinal scan and they walked along the metal-sheathed hallway. Dot brushed aside the last of her amusement and became serious as they approached a solid slab of metal.

Made of a mixture of aluminum, platinum, and silver, it looked more like a dead end than a door. There were no palm and retinal scanners and keypads here, nor any seams, hinges, or handles. The only sign it was something special were the glowing gold sigils etched upon every inch of its surface. The entrance to the library's dangerous books section was magical and required a very special kind of key to enter.

Chloe and Dot threaded out their individual wills, intertwining them much like a weaver at a loom. The pattern and tempo of the magical dance was so complex that Wilson couldn't keep track of whose will was where at any given time. Once the door was covered with the metaphysical cloth of their making, the twins simultaneously pressed a sequence of sigils, continuously changing time signatures but always in sync with each other.

Even though there was no moving parts, the door groaned as it became translucent, allowing them passage to the other side. Each librarian placed a hand on Wilson as they entered, keying him to the door for this visit. Had they not, he wouldn't be allowed to leave—there was no key from the other side.

The repository was a large open gallery forty feet wide and 300 feet deep. Solid pillars of salt rose from the floor to support the ten-foot tall ceiling. There were no open shelves or clearly labeled tomes here, just row after row of huts built out of large salt bricks plastered over with a thick brine that was as strong as masonry when hardened and cured. Each hut was identical in size and appearance—they were the equivalent of solitary confinement for dangerous magical books. Each hut had its own warded door made of powder-coated aluminum etched with silver sigils. Wilson couldn't perceive any difference from one to another, but the librarians knew each saline building's inhabitants.

"Follow us," Chloe said without any pleasantries or lightness. The twins were all business now. The traces of vanilla and leather of the stacks outside were absent, replaced by a briny aroma. Even the air contained minuscule particles of salt, sprayed into circulation by the repository's custom ventilation system. It reminded Wilson of the sea only this was hardly a jaunt to the beach. He'd already been esoterically had once today, and he didn't want a repeat.

They stopped at the saline hut that housed *Liber Odores* and the twins once again wove their will together, but in a less complex manner. Wilson could follow the pattern and rhythm this time, but it would be impossible for a single person to reproduce it. The door swung out, opening on silent hinges. The inside was only ten feet square and had the bare essentials: a small wooden table with two chairs, two banker's lamps to read by, and a sigiled bookshelf that housed the books.

Despite its title, *Liber Odores* was actually multiple volumes that were considered a singular work, like the Oxford English Dictionary. It was created sometime in the early 600s by Arnulf of Metz and found its way to Baghdad in the late 800s where Abu Yūsuf Ya'qūb ibn 'Isḥāq aṣ-Ṣabbāḥ al-Kindī expanded upon it. It traveled along the Silk Road, where Al-Biruni found it in Bukhara in the early 1000s and made significant additions, but after that, its history became murky.

It eventually resurfaced in France in the 1590s where renowned chemist Jean Beguin took up its mantel and broadened its scope further. Once in Europe, it changed hands among the various European noble houses until it crossed the Atlantic and wound up in New York in 1910. By then, it had grown to eighteen volumes, the last fatally begun by Imro Fox. After his death, *Liber Odores* was dispersed throughout America and Europe as part of his estate. Fifteen of the eighteen volumes now resided in the dangerous books repository on the wooden bookshelf standing in front of Wilson.

Wilson took a seat at the table, leaving the oversized chair for Chloe and Dot. They went to the bookshelf and pulled out the first volume—the keystone needed to make deposits. It was essentially the *Liber Odores* scent index, where it checked to make sure it didn't already contain the aroma before creating a new entry plucked from the memory of the user.

"Don't touch it yet," Dot cautioned as they set the book down and situated themselves at the table. Wilson heeded the warning. Even though this wasn't his first time accessing it, he was far from blasé about the danger. *Liber Odores* may have been created to collect smells, but it was hungry for any memories, not just olfactory ones. That was what landed it a place in the dangerous books repository and how the librarians had put so much of its history together: accessing the additional memories the book had acquired over time.

Dot took the lead while Chloe took the role of tether. "Before you touch the book, clear your mind and focus on the smell you wish to identify. Don't name it. Don't give it environmental context in any other way than olfactory." She'd given him the exact same speech twice before. While both had eidetic memories, only Dot repeated herself in precisely the same way every time. Once she found how she wanted to say something, she found no reason to deviate while Chloe liked to mix things up.

"I've done this before," he reminded her, even though he knew full well she already knew that. "I know what I'm doing."

"You also know how to protect yourself from charms," Dot chided him. There was no dry sarcasm or humorous dig in her statement, only concern. Wilson took her point and closed his eyes, cutting away the visions of putrefied flesh, the colorful wings of butterflies fluttering en mass, and Anderson's silky blonde hair and silvery eyes. He nodded when he held just the essence of the aroma that had so far eluded him.

Dot opened the tome and instructed him further. "Place

your hands on the book. It will try to pull the memory from your mind. Let it, but break contact once the memory is gone."

Wilson reached out and placed his fingertips on the vellum. An arcane charge sparked as he made contact. Skin on skin, *Liber Odores* was drawn to the memory. It felt like standing in front of an airlock that had just been opened. Against all his instincts, he loosened his hold on the memory. Magic always had its price, and this time, it was his to pay.

A thin wisp of smoke spiraled out of the center of his forehead and dribbled away into the pages of the book. When he could no longer recall the floral notes, he retracted his hands from the page and slapped his will over his third eye. Dot pushed the book away to put more physical space between it and Wilson, and Chloe dropped a cleaver of her will to sever any lingering connection between them.

The most dangerous part was over, and they entered the tedious phase: the waiting. It could take anywhere from seconds to hours to get a result. The librarians didn't know how *Liber Odores* operated on an algorithmic level, but they knew it would tell them where the entry was in the larger work, like a magical card catalogue. If the scent was novel, it would send them to the new entry made in the last volume, which the Salt Mine had in its possession. If it was already known, it would show the location of the pre-exiting entry. In that case, Wilson just had to hope it wasn't in one of the missing volumes.

They kept the chatter to a minimum—it was never wise to

give dangerous books more information than was absolutely necessary. Eventually, a notation appeared on the page. It was in an archaic script but the librarians knew how to decipher it.

"You're in luck," Chloe told Wilson. "It's in one of the volumes we have." He stayed seated while the twins returned Volume 1 and pulled Volume 8 off the shelf; in the repository, visitors didn't handle the books unless explicitly told to do so.

Between their four hands, Chloe and Dot tracked down the entry. "Narcissus Flower, also known as Titania's Daffodil," they reported. Wilson said nothing but beamed at obtaining a definitive result. While he no longer had the specific memory of the scent, he knew the plant that dotted the Magh Meall. He wasn't much of a flowers guy, but even he had to admit they were breathtakingly beautiful; their namesake in the mortal realm couldn't hold a flame to the real thing.

They came in many different colors—sometimes making them hard to properly identify—but regardless of hue and slight variation in form, all were slightly narcotic. It was one of the reasons Wilson never stopped to smell the flowers in the Magh Meall, although they didn't really pose much of a threat except when encountered in large numbers. Their unique qualities made them a base ingredient in the more powerful charm potions, dusts, and unguents.

Wilson never had cause to seek out such things. He wasn't much of an alchemist—making magical concoctions was simultaneously too precise and imprecise for his liking—but he knew it could be found on the Magh Meall's black market. It took a lot of flowers to distill enough essence and in some regions, harvesting them was a punishable offense because it was the favored flower of Titania, an imperial figure amongst the fae.

The librarians put the book back on the shelf, and they left the saline hut in the same condition they'd found it. They closed the aluminum door and locked it with a different arcane pattern, sealing the contents inside the shell of magically inert salt. Wilson noted this pattern could be done by a single practitioner. The repository door was no longer translucent but they were able to pass through it nonetheless. Wilson shuttered at the thought of being trapped in the saline tomb with all those books.

LaSalle was waiting for them outside the repository door. His long form leaned against the wall as he tapped away on his tablet. His tie was loosened and his suit bore the signs of a long day. "Any luck?"

"Narcissus Flower," Wilson answered him triumphantly as they all made their way back to the circular desk.

"You think that's how she charmed you?" Chloe put forth a theory.

"Maybe, but I searched her things the first time I knocked her out. You'd think I would have noticed something like that," Wilson hedged.

"But if you were already charmed by then…" Dot spoke up

and felt no need to complete the sentence.

"I didn't find any on her person or in her possessions," LaSalle added.

"What did you find?" Wilson asked curiously.

"I found the tracer and removed it. I think that's how the Dökkálfar and the mantid hit squad found her," he said with clipped precision. "But I've got nothing beyond that."

They stared at him. "What do you mean, nothing?" Chloe said delicately.

"I can't process her," LaSalle stated flatly. His cool demeanor was showing cracks. "She's not human, at least not entirely human, but she's definitely got some human in there." Wilson found it unnerving to watch LaSalle struggle to explain his nebulous findings within his normally rigid parameters. The guy was a rock, and he didn't like anything that rattled LaSalle.

Dot tossed him a bottle of water when they arrived at the desk and LaSalle took a long drink. "One more time, with clarity?" Chloe patiently nudged.

The towering man took a seat and tried using more words. "When I process someone, I'm basically making a map of their unconscious and dream-state consciousness—what's going on behind the scenes before the higher executive functions of the frontal cortex get involved. It's like walking in the halls of their mind. In that setting, magical alterations stick out and can be removed or remediated." Wilson listened intently—LaSalle wasn't the talkative sort and the metaphysics of the process had always been a black box to him.

"Everyone's map looks different, unique to them, but in humans, they are always square corridors. For all the chaos and drama they like to create in their lives, humans crave order at their core. Except parts of Anderson's map aren't square. Some are oval and no matter how I approach those sections, I can't travel within them. They are warded against me," he said incredulously. "That's not supposed to happen."

"Have you tried a different approach—a proverbial back door?" Dot spit-balled.

LaSalle ran with her analogy. "I've tried the back door, the kitchen window, the second-story balcony, and the chimney. Every time I get close, I get redirected or lost. I had to start the process three times before I'd finally mapped all her square corridors and even some of those don't connect with each other. As far as I can tell, the oval passages are the only connections between the fragments of her human consciousness."

"Could she be an advanced practitioner?" Wilson asked, wondering if he'd been very cleverly duped from the beginning.

LaSalle shook his head. "No, she's not a practitioner."

Wilson guffawed. "I've *seen* her use magic. *Killing* magic."

LaSalle straightened at the insinuation and steeled his voice "The parts that I can reach show no magical aptitude. If she used magic, it's coming from the parts that aren't human."

"Everything points to fae," Chloe stated the obvious.

"Except she passed the cold iron test," Wilson interjected.

"For me as well," LaSalle corroborated. Without knowing when Wilson had been compromised, LaSalle had retested everything Wilson had reported as fact.

LaSalle pulled out a plastic bag from the inner pocket of his suit and handed it to Wilson. "Leader's in Washington and can't be here until morning, but she wants you to find out as much information as you can on Anderson. We need to nail down precisely what we're dealing with here."

Wilson took the locks of honey blonde hair and nodded. He knew what that meant—time for some serious summoning. "Check's in the mail?" he asked, referring to the costly karmic debt he would incur.

"Preapproved," LaSalle affirmed. Then he turned to Chloe and Dot. "She wants you two to take a look at her and see if you see anything I've missed."

"Give us fifteen minutes to secure things here," Chloe answered for the pair.

LaSalle nodded. "I'll be waiting outside the room." The two men left the twins and walked silently to the elevator. Neither were prone to fill the quiet with mindless chatter. However, the irony was too much for LaSalle. In the long ride to the top, a small smile crept onto his lips. "Narcissus flower. Not something you encounter every day."

Wilson didn't say anything. A certain amount of ribbing was expected.

Chapter Fifteen

Detroit, Michigan, USA
9th of March, 11:34 p.m. (GMT-5)

Wilson pulled in front of his garage door for the second time that night, except this time there were no esoteric alarms blaring in his brain and he was able to easily steer his 911 into his normal parking space. He waited until the steel jaws of the garage door sealed the 500 before heading upstairs to immediately undress, putting his clothes aside to be laundered before showering. If there was any lingering scent on him, he wanted to be rid of it as it was unwise to bring any baggage into a summoning, literally or metaphorically. He let the hot water wash over him and breathed in the vapor. It had been a long day but he wasn't done yet.

When he exited the steamy bathroom with a towel around his thin waist, he found Mau sprawled on the bed, batting at the baggie containing Megan Anderson's hair. Her emerald eyes lit up with each smack as she knocked it from one paw to another.

"I'd prefer you didn't do that. I need it for work," he simply stated his preference. He didn't try to issue orders to Mau. The ebony cat directed her green eyes to him and saw he'd had a rough day. He smelled different and the blackness around him slinked instead of crawled.

She was not one to do as she was told, but she knew being considerate to his petty requests from time to time was also important. Something in her eyes changed as she deliberately pawed it one more time before abandoning it. She was over it anyway.

"Thank you," he said politely and rewarded her civility with a well-placed scratch behind her ears on his way to retrieve the hair sample. He placed it on one of his nearby bookshelves and started dressing. "I'm going to be in the summoning room for a while. Is there anything you need before I go?"

Mau meowed like a normal cat, but pushed a *no* to Crawling Shadow's query. She wasn't always so communicative, but she'd been treating him with kid gloves since last week. He had many questions that she could not answer for him, but she could at least attest to her personal satiety. He worked best with certainty.

She gathered on her haunches and then leapt into the air, disappearing at the apex of the arc. Wilson had seen it many times before and was accustomed to Mau doing as she pleased. She wasn't so much his cat as he was her human. He was tying the laces of his shoes when she returned to the bed, carrying her own small plastic bag in her mouth. She dropped it on the bed and started batting at that. Wilson tucked the hair sample into his pocket and left the cat to her amusements.

The mundane living space of his fourth-floor apartment within the converted warehouse was only 1,000 square feet, a fraction of the 8,000 circumscribed but the building's outer walls. Before his visit with Baba Yaga and his stay in Avalon, he'd limited his practice to those disciplines that didn't make him high as kite. With Chloe and Dot's tutelage, he discovered he had a real talent for summoning, as the preparation and attention to detail suited his temperament. Thus, when it came time to build his very own fortress of solitude, he'd dedicated 3,000 square feet to summoning.

Naturally, it had to be hidden from the rest of the house, so he'd sequestered it via a cold iron door inlaid with silver sigils. Behind that, a short hallway led to a personal gym and a fully stocked S&M dungeon—the first he only used occasionally and the later not at all. Blurring the lines between pleasure and pain wasn't his particular kink, but it served as a plausible red herring for anyone curious about the ornate door and the complex sequence of four handles to open it.

Wilson walked past the racks of toys, restraints, and specialized equipment until he came to the massive Saint Andrew's Cross that was bolted to the floor of the dungeon. He climbed it and felt for the release catch at the very top. With a pull of his fingertips, he freed the cross from the bolts that held it in place and revealed a dark crawlspace behind it. It was a tight fit made a little more comfortable after he'd lost all his bulk in Avalon.

It was pitch black when he reached the end. He stood and oriented himself in the right direction, taking precisely the correct number of steps to the light switch on the other side of the room. As a soft glow flooded the study, he passed the cherry wood bookshelves and made a beeline to the lone ebony one paned with sheets of pure quartz and inlaid with ivory sign and sigils.

It was mostly empty, containing only twenty-seven books, and it didn't take him long to find the title he was looking for: *The Recurved Mind of Elliot Smith.* Once he had it in hand, he closed the case and took a seat at the baroque reading desk. He turned on the Emeralite desk lamp with a light tug on its chain, decorated to look like a string of miniature golden apples.

The slim book was the biography and case study of a young man driven to insanity during the First World War. His doctor had come to the conclusion that the angels and devils his patient saw were manifestations of psychological damage, but Wilson suspected that Elliot Smith was really seeing supernatural beings. On a hunch, he'd liberated the dusty and neglected work from a shuttered library in a small town among the rolling hills of eastern Ohio. Time and study had proven him correct. Wilson flipped to the exhaustive endnotes in the back until the spine fell open to same spread he referred to each time he summoned the Smile in the Darkness.

While Wilson generally avoided summoning demons,

Smile was the exception to the rule. It lacked the creativity and native cunning so common to demons and it was easily bribed for one of its stature. Smile had yet to lead Wilson astray, although not for lack of trying. It just wasn't that bright. It was big, powerful, direct, dumb, and knowledgeable, which made it perfect for extracting information from as long as a practitioner was skilled enough to keep it in bonds during the summoning.

The only real downside to summoning the Smile in the Darkness was the fact that it was a blood eater. Smile was hungry and everything was food. Once it had the taste of a person, bits of it could seep out of whatever blasted wasteland was its natural realm and follow them around, causing havoc that would eventually result in their death.

To counteract this, Wilson spent quite a bit of karma to metaphysically remove the scent trail after each summoning, and that was all he needed to hit the reset button. However, the last time he'd summoned Smile—more than a year ago now—the demon had started to put it together. It didn't remember Wilson, but it had remembered that it'd tasted him before. Wilson had doubled down on the ritual scrubbing and hoped it was enough, but he was about to find out.

Wilson moved into the adjoining room—the summoning chamber. It was the largest of his secret rooms and the floor was inlaid with six different types of summoning and protective circles. The only furniture was a single wooden chair used by Cotton Mather during the Salem Witch Trials and a long cabineted table upon which resided various occult objects. Next to the table was a mini-fridge in which Wilson kept perishables. In the past, he took blood samples every two months and used a centrifuge and a dollop of magic to keep it fresh, but he had since stopped the practice just in case the preservation magic was what tipped Smile off the last time. Plus, when summoning a blood eater, the fresher the better.

He attached an 18-gauge needle to a syringe and wiped down his arm with an alcohol swab before applying the tourniquet. He pumped his hand a few times, making a fist and releasing it until a plump vein popped out. He pulled 5 cc of blood before pulling out the needle and releasing the tie around his upper arm.

Once he was sure the bleeding had stopped, he entered the thirteen-sided star inscribed by a great circle and emptied the contents of the syringe onto a smaller darkly stained circle that lay in its center. Then he dropped in a few strands of Anderson's hair on the sticky crimson, linking the offering with the service.

Wilson placed the wooden chair beside the tridecagram and summoned his will. *Think, think, think...* Then, he recited Smith's poem.

The tree in winter dreams of spring.
The root in spring dreams of rain.
The leaf in summer dreams of flying away.

And I, in prayer, dream of the smile in the darkness.

"I summon you," he intoned, and then repeated the poem. "I summon you," he chanted a second time, again repeating the poem. His final "I summon you" brought the Smile in the Darkness into the mortal realm as the tridecagram filled with whirling, black smoke.

The psychic assault of Smile's presence, even when contained within his impeccable circle, made Wilson's monkey mind shriek in terror; he immediately wanted to hide in the corner and fling poo. He steeled himself and waited, actively working on keeping every part of him inscrutable to the demon's perception. It never paid to seem too eager in a summoning.

Eventually, Smile stridulated, "I am here." It was comprehensible but decidedly not a voice.

"I require service of you," Wilson responded, using the same script he'd used in previous summonings; like Dot, he didn't believe there was a reason to change things up when he knew what worked.

The smoke spoke. "The sacrifice?"

"Hidden from your view. I will now reveal it, but you can only consume it if you agree." Wilson raised an arm and allowed the demon to see the blood and hair.

From the darkness, needle-sharp teeth as long as Wilson's forearm appeared, sticking out of a cartilaginous jaw. There were no discernable features of a face, but the maw bent forward and somehow sniffed it nonetheless. "David Emrys Wilson, the scent-hider and the path-obscurer, is known to me," it said prosaically. Wilson superficially kept his cool while he reinforced the circle with more of his will. It was never good when a demon remembered one's name.

"But this is different," it declared with interest as it inhaled the scent of Anderson's hair. "This is *new*." The floating jaw salivated. "The question?"

"Two questions," Wilson proffered, banking on its apparent excitement. His attempted negotiation was met with thousands of tiny piranha-like jaws that jetted out of the smoke. A wave of teeth crashed against the magic restraining Smile.

"The wards are good," Wilson said calmly, even as his heart raced. "Two questions for two offerings."

"Agreed!" boomed out of the smoke. The massive jaw of a megaladon appeared with Wilson's blood coating its yellowing teeth. Meanwhile, the swarm of piranha jaws chewed on the hair until it turned into honey-blonde smoke that was subsumed by the blackness. A vibration filled the darkness, like the hum of distant children happily playing. Wilson let it enjoy its meal, and when it was finished, it spoke again. "What is the first question?"

"What is the nature of this creature?" Wilson annunciated crisply. The jaws smirked. "This is not a creature."

God, I hate demons, Wilson thought to himself. He knew Smile wasn't lying. Regardless of their nature, once a summoned creature entered into an agreement, they were magically bound and forced by a summoner's will to comply. Smile could only twist and elide the truth, not state blatant falsehoods.

"I assure you it comes from one subject," he asserted in hopes of getting more information out of Smile without using the second question. He'd long learned phrasing counts when dealing with summoned beings.

"You assure me falsely because you perceive falsely." Smile growled. Wilson didn't know how a jaw could look so smug, but it did. No one liked to be condescended to, especially demons who knew they weren't the sharpest tool in the shed.

The gears in his head were churning. Smile was telling *some* version of the truth, and he just had to suss out enough to make the most out of his final question. Creature was an all-inclusive term, which was why he'd used that word specifically, but Smile was somehow putting Anderson outside of that classification. According to LaSalle, she was human plus something else with all other signs pointing to fae except that she'd been cold iron tested as empirically not fae.

Wilson focused on Smile's last words: you perceive falsely. If Wilson could not trust his own senses, he could rely on his wards. They saw everything, including the unseen and visually imperceptible. He considered the alarms Anderson had triggered. LaSalle had removed a tracer and Wilson made an executive decision to set aside the fae alarm for the time being. That left the final ward Anderson had triggered: one against ghosts. It was designed to keep out the ethereal beings as well as people possessed by ghosts.

Obviously, Anderson wasn't a ghost or possessed by one—LaSalle would have worked that out in seconds during a deep processing—but what if she mimicked that state? What if she was multiple creatures that just looked like one creature? He knocked the idea around and found it sound. It fit all the pieces of information he knew as well as what Smile had said to him.

While he thought, Smile had become bored of waiting in its cage and was sending out multiple mouths, each jeering and making unsavory suggestions on what it would do with Wilson's soul when it devoured him.

Wilson gave the demon his full attention and made another statement of fact. "I know this creature is fae and human." He knew he was on the right track when suddenly all the voices from the smoke quieted and the floating maws disappeared. "Here is my second and final question: were I to seek all of this not-creature, in how many places would I look?"

The blackness completely stilled and formed a solid cylinder within the tridecagram. A small set of human jaws emerged, no bigger than a toddler's. "Two," it said petulantly.

With the agreement fulfilled, all of the smoke and darkness disappeared as the connection was severed and Smile in the Darkness was shunted out of the mortal realm. Even though Wilson knew the monster was gone, his brain was still flush with endorphins and adrenaline so he took advantage of his state and performed a deluxe ritual scrubbing, burning through karma at an incredible rate. Smile may have remembered his name, but that didn't mean it could trace him yet.

He fought back exhaustion long enough to put everything away and return to the mundane portion of the 500. Once on the other side of the cold iron door, he gave LaSalle the go ahead to make the sizable donation to one of Wilson's chosen children's hospitals. Seeing that all was as he'd expected, he updated LaSalle and by association, the librarians—maybe they could make some sense of it. Wilson was in the kitchen downing a full glass of water when his phone buzzed. It was LaSalle. *Get some sleep. We'll deal with this tomorrow. 07:00 update.*

It was blessed news and instead of making an espresso, he set it for the morning. He could have pushed through if he had to, but he would gladly take the rest. In the bedroom, Mau was still on the mattress, batting away at a different makeshift toy. Even though they did not exchange words or thoughts, they moved in a choreographed fashion. She moved to make space for him while he undressed. Wilson drew back the comforter and climbed in, leaving the flap open. Mau crawled under the covers and nestled alongside him and they slept.

Chapter Sixteen

Detroit, Michigan, USA
10th of March, 6:01 a.m. (GMT-5)

The rumble of the postal service trucks roused Wilson from his slumber. Mau was nowhere to be seen and Megan Anderson's face was in his mind's eye. He tried to chalk it up to the complexity of the case, but what he was experiencing wasn't cranial in nature. It was more like empathy. It wasn't so long ago that his body had housed two souls. At least the second soul in his body was another human's—a fragment of someone who loved him and who'd done something extraordinary to save his life. There had been no way for either of them to know what would unfold from that singular heroic act. Wilson couldn't begin to imagine what it must feel like to share a body with the spirit of a fae.

He'd be tempted to chalk it up to being charmed if he didn't know better—if LaSalle said he fixed it, it was fixed. He threw back the covers and pulled the rug out from under his swelling emotions before they could gain momentum. He was still on the case, and getting emotional wouldn't help. This wasn't about him; it was about making sense of the butterfly deaths, and preferably ending them.

He started doing his usual stretches and calisthenics, and eventually his mind cleared as his blood started pumping. Even though he had just showered last night, he took another, partially out of habit but also because he wanted to wash away the encounter with the Smile in the Darkness. He toweled off and selected a tailored suit from his closet. The smell of coffee wafted into his bedroom just as he was straightening his tie into a perfect Windsor.

"Good morning, Mau," he addressed the Sphinx-like form resting next to her feeding station. She acknowledged his presence by reaching out one paw toward the empty bowl and tapping twice. Wilson obliged and popped a can of tuna into the silver and gold bowl.

As she downed her food with her usual gusto—she made growly noises when she ate—he washed his hands of any lingering tuna juice before grabbing his espressos. His phone buzzed with a message from LaSalle: *07:30 meeting*. That could only mean one thing: Leader was back in town and she had a plan. He put down his mobile and made eggs and toast for breakfast. Something told him he was going to need his strength.

Wilson had enough time to deposit his possessions in his subterranean office on the fifth floor before catching the elevator to the fourth floor. LaSalle was at his desk, clean-shaven and in a fresh suit. "Good morning, Fulcrum. Leader will be with you in a minute." The brick of a man was all business as usual and any trace of friendly camaraderie that may have passed between them last night was gone.

When the time hit half past, Wilson rose with LaSalle and followed him to Leader's office door. Leader was seated at her desk in a posture of contemplation, her eyes filled with the wistful glaze of someone looking into the distant past, a faraway place, or both. She was back in her normal attire today, a pair of well-worn jeans and a thick, natural wool sweater she'd knitted herself many years ago. After a series of meetings in Washington, she was glad to be back in her real clothes. She understood the need for optics, but that didn't make it any less tedious.

Her gray eyes recovered their piercing intensity as soon as the door opened. "Fulcrum, please take a seat," Leader said as he walked in. Despite her petite stature and casual dress, sitting opposite her felt like stepping in front of the prow of an icebreaker and he was the ice.

There were no files pulled from the bank of cabinets behind her and no stacks of paperwork in either the in or out basket. The only thing on her massive desktop was a small, square wooden box. Instead of returning to his desk, LaSalle stayed in the room and closed the door behind them. Wilson's curiosity was piqued at the deviation from standard operating procedure but quietly took a seat in one of the white oversized leather chairs.

Leader sat forward and pushed the box toward Wilson. "I'm sending you to retrieve something. You'll need this."

Wilson took that as an invitation to pick it up. The box wasn't lead lined or packed with salt. It wasn't even covered in containment runes. It was just a plain sandalwood box, albeit one ornately carved in an ivy motif that he gently fingered as he opened it.

Inside was a copper object that resembled a compass, except that it had two hands which were slowly spinning in opposite directions. On each of the hands was an ivory pip at its tip.

"Looks dwarven," he took a guess. The dwarves loved to work in copper. The one dwarven home he'd visited was filled with the red metal, gleaming in the hearth flames.

"Correct. It's a dwarven compass used to find *grárglóa* veins," she filled in the gaps for him.

Wilson's heart skipped a beat. "Grárglóa, as in the magical metal that is sharper than steel and nearly indestructible?" he asked.

"The very same," she confirmed. Once it sunk in how precious the item in his hand was, he carefully put it back on its padded, silk-lined perch in the box. Only the dwarves could find the rare silvery gray metal with any reliability and working it was a closely guarded Dwarven secret. In the metal-poor Magh Meall, it was nearly a hundred times more valuable than gold, the other metal the dwarves were obsessed with.

"Weber has modified it to find the second part of whatever

is inhabiting Megan Anderson. Once you are outside the Mine, one of the dials will stop spinning and steer you in the right direction. The closer you get, the closer the ivory bead will move toward the center of the dial. Once you're on top of it, that bead will glow red," she explained.

"And the other will keep spinning because Anderson is in the Mine?" Wilson extrapolated. The slight nod Leader gave him lit him up, like a schoolchild who got the answer right in front of the whole class.

Wilson closed the box and secured it in his breast pocket. "Parameters?"

"Once you find it, bring it back. Lancer will be assisting you, but you'll retain lead. You'll be going as Discretion Minerals. We want to stay off the radar on this one but if you get in a jam, you can use your FBI credentials and we'll provide cover," she answered and checked her wristwatch. "Lancer should have the truck ready. David gave her the broad strokes but you'll have to finish briefing her on route. She has all your cover documentation."

Leader didn't have to tell him why Lancer was coming. He'd gotten charmed once and it was harder to charm two people. Wilson knew it was the smart operational decision and swallowed his pride.

"What exactly are we looking for?" he asked for more details.

A queer look blinked across Leader's face. It was almost a

smile but it was gone before Wilson could pin it down. "You'll know it when you see it."

Wilson nodded; he'd reached the end of his need to know. Obviously, Anderson was in the middle of some affair between the Dökkálfar and House Tantali, and Leader had an opinion on the relationship she wasn't willing to share. He was fine with that: fae politics was a giant bag of worms, and on this occasion, he was content to do the work without sticking his hand into the squirming sack.

Chapter Seventeen

Detroit, Michigan, USA
10th of March, 7:58 a.m. (GMT-5)

A front loader was depositing four tons of premium rock salt into the back of a small box truck as Wilson approached with his attaché in one hand and standard issue Salt Mine luggage in the other. From the outside, the truck looked completely normal: a work vehicle covered in a persistent film of road filth from constant use. However, he knew this truck to be special. The box frame was etched with sigils concealed by internal cladding, and the space between the cladding and the frame was packed with salt. Effectively, it was a giant containment box on wheels. The additional salt being placed inside was more for both visually obscuring the actual payload once he found it and neutralizing its magic.

He waved as he spotted Martinez standing beside the driver's side door. Dressed in one of her pantsuits paired with low-heeled boots, she could easily make the pivot from businesswoman to G-man with a few minor adjustments. They exchanged perfunctory pleasantries and played their respective roles—Davis Watson and Tessa Marvel, Director and Assistant

Director of Acquisitions of Discretion Minerals—for the benefit of the mundane workers onsite.

After the mini-excavator was loaded into the truck, they climbed aboard; two high-level executives wooing potential clients by getting their hands dirty. The mission packet was already inside the cab and included six manifests, each with a different end destination: four crafted for USA inspection and two in case they crossed the border into Canada. Once outside of the Salt Mine's wards, one of the compass's needles pointed north-northeast but the ivory pip was still far from its center. There was no telling how far they would have to travel once they got moving.

After loading up, they faced the I-94 East onramp with Martinez behind the wheel and Wilson playing navigator. Unfortunately, they were in the worst of rush hour traffic and there was little chitchat as she steered the cargo truck onto the highway. It was a far cry from the muscle cars she was fond of driving, but she managed to find a gap traveling at a steady pace in the slow lane.

She caught sight of the shiny compass in Wilson's hands in her peripheral vision. It looked different that the one she'd used before to track down rakshasas with Liu—codename Aurora—but the Salt Mine's resident inventor and quartermaster never was one to rest on his laurels. He was always improving and tweaking his creations.

"Did Weber make a new compass?" she asked, signaling

it was safe to engage in discussion without threat of vehicular collision.

"No, it's actually a dwarven compass that he jerry-rigged to help us find what we are looking for," Wilson replied with one eye on the compass needle and the other on the atlas. Dwarves were regarded as precision craftsmen, and he was watching the pip for any sign of movement to see if he could establish a correlation between its movement and distance traveled on the road.

"What exactly are we looking for?" she probed, hoping he knew because she didn't have a clue.

He shrugged. "Don't know, but considering they gave us the truck and enough salt to neutralize a magical pachyderm, I'm guessing it's big. Did LaSalle give you any hints?"

She shook her head. "No, but I don't think he knows either."

That made Wilson take his eyes off the compass and scan her profile—she was on the level. "What makes you say that?"

She wobbled her head side to side. "Something about the way he didn't answer my questions."

"He *did* stay in Leader's office during my briefing this morning," he thoughtfully submitted his own piece of evidence. "What would she be after that she didn't tell her right-hand man about?"

Martinez made a noncommittal gesture without taking her hands off the wheel. Working with incomplete information was something she was used to and she was here as operational support. She just needed to know enough to get the job done and not to get her or Wilson killed.

"Why don't you fill me in on what you do know," she recommended. His audible exhale suggested it was a doozey.

"You want the short or long version?" he asked.

"Give me the elevator speech and we'll go from there," she said whimsically.

He paused and tried to sum up the situation as concisely as possible. "We're looking for the second half of a creature—probably fae—that is inhabiting the body of a twenty-four-year-old actress who is killing people by shooting a rainbow from her hand."

Martinez merely nodded; there was a time when that sentence would have been weird. "She been in anything I might have seen?"

He smirked—he'd forgotten how funny she could be. "Probably not. Couple of commercials and bit parts on TV."

She eyed a whizzing gnat of a compact car making overtures of cutting her off and liberally laid on the horn. "Yeah, asshole, I can't stop this thing on a dime—stay in your lane!"

When the other driver eased off and respected her space, she returned her attention to Wilson. "So when you say rainbow, do you mean a literal one—like a lethal Care Bear stare?"

"Yes, but I doubt there is a Care Bear that can melt people and have the corpse blister and pop out butterflies while exuding the fragrance of narcissus flowers," he elaborated on the odd mechanism of death. "I mean, even I would have watched *that* show."

She snorted. He was at least a decade older than her and the idea of him watching the Care Bears was too comical.

"Is that how you got charmed?" she asked gingerly.

Of course LaSalle told her that part, he grumbled to himself. "No, that came later but the same odor was there."

"These things happen," she said automatically. "That's why we go in pairs into the Magh Meall. There's nothing wrong with someone covering your back."

"I go into the Magh Meall by myself all the time," he rebutted.

"And you also got charmed," she pointed out.

"For your information, I got charmed here," he corrected her before realizing that really wasn't any better optics.

Her brow furrowed. "How did enough narcissus flowers get here to charm you? Alicia and I didn't have any trouble until we ran into a whole meadow of them."

"There weren't any flowers, just the smell," he replied. "Apparently, butterflies love it."

She could tell she'd hit a nerve and offered an olive branch. "I got you something. It's in the sack behind me."

His eyebrow rose at the non sequitur and he reached behind her seat. A genuine grin came across his face when he pulled out a bag of ranch corn nuts.

“I was going to save it for later but it sounds like you could use a win,” she drily remarked. “And there’s also a packet of breath mints in there. For after.”

He set the package aside for the time being and began briefing her in full. Coming in on a mission-in-progress wasn’t a cakewalk for either parties, and forewarned was forearmed. He expounded in his characteristic, straightforward delivery—just the facts, ma’am—and she made signs that she was listening while driving. She was glad Wilson was back to his normal self, otherwise this was going to be a long scavenger hunt.

By the time he was finished, they were miles down M-25 and the deep blue of Lake Huron rippled on their right, but the ivory pip was still far from the compass’s center. When they reached the end of the line in Forestville, MI, Martinez pulled over. “Could it be in the water?”

He sighed. “If it is, we’ve brought a knife to a gunfight.” He expanded the map until it covered the entire dashboard and eyeballed a straight line from Detroit to their current bearing and extrapolated it across the Lake Huron until it once again hit land: Manitoulin Island.

She grabbed her phone and typed it in with her thumbs. “There isn’t a ferry this time of year and this thing’s definitely not amphibious.”

He traced a path with his finger on the map. While the compass pointed as the crow flies, they were limited to roads. It was one hell of a circuitous route through the Upper Peninsula into Canada, but there was a bridge that connected the island to the mainland. He looked at the time on his Girard-Perregaux and did some mental math.

"Let's check it out. If we get there and the compass points to the water, we'll have to regroup anyway," he said once he'd made up his mind.

"You're lead," she assented without resistance. It was a long drive but she would have made the same call in his shoes. She put the truck into gear and pulled off the shoulder. "But I get to pick the music."

"Fine by me," he agreed and opened his bag of corn nuts.

"What icon would a killer Care Bear have on its belly?" she asked, opening the door for hours of mindless road games to come. "I have to think skull and bones would be a little too on the nose."

He popped a savory morsel into his mouth and played along. "Maybe, but think of the merch! Slap an eye patch and a triangle hat on it and brand it as a Pirate Bear."

Many contemplations of such importance were explored as they drove north. Even though he didn't actively seek it out outside of work, he didn't mind passing time with Martinez. They had spent a lot of time together during her training and had gotten used to being in each other's company. She had an impeccable knack for making conversation without actually having to talk about anything substantial. It made killing time and necessary tasks less tedious.

Eventually, he was able to make a rough guess on their target's general location using some basic geometry and how far down the pip had slid down the needle. They cheered when it looked like their prize was on land, even though it meant they had to keep driving.

They switched roles after lunch and crossed the border without incident. Once they were on Canadian soil, falling back on their FBI badges became less useful, but they were both cautious by nature. Their motto was don't get caught. Eventually the needle pointed to the south leaving only one possibility: Manitoulin Island.

It was the world's largest freshwater island, but it didn't appear to be much different than the rest of Canada that bordered the Great Lakes. Successive generations had cleared much of the natural forest and now it was a solid mix of farm and woods with the occasional lot given up to cattle or horses. Neither of them had been before, and Martinez bought a more detailed map when they stopped at a local gas station to fill the tank.

Wilson drove onto island as the sun was low on the horizon, cutting in and out through the intermittent tall pine and maple trees that lined the side of the road. Martinez had to hold up her hand and look between her fingers to read the old signs.

"I think we just passed Pike Lake," she informed Wilson, who couldn't see against the sun and drive at the same time. She looked down at the compass on top of the paper map she'd folded to isolate this section of the island. "And the ivory dot is nearly at the center." The needle swung abruptly as they drove past a white graveled road. "Wait! That was our turn on the right."

He brought the truck to a stop, put it in reverse, and took the turn. Once the needle and the front end of their vehicle were in alignment, Martinez made another dash on the map. The next few miles were slow going, but they were boxing it in with each turn. It didn't help that there were few landmarks—and even fewer signs—and the roads never went the way they needed.

After another half hour of abrupt stops and turns, Martinez triumphantly circled the real estate in question: a field the size of a football field bordered by trees.

"The good news is that I know where we need to go," she started optimistically. "But there aren't any roads leading in. This is as close as we're getting in the truck."

Wilson pulled over and stopped the truck. The seats weren't terribly comfortable; after hours of driving, the prospect of going on foot didn't seem that bad. "Then we better make the most of what light we have left."

They slipped on oversized mud boots and left the box truck with shovels in hand. They jumped a drainage ditch and made sure the wire fence wasn't electrified before clambering over.

"This has gotta be the right place," she insisted. "It's a perfect country landscape. All it needs is a couple of cows chewing cud and a babbling stream."

He kept his eyes on the compass but the corners of his mouth upturned. "A little *too* quiet and serene?" He stopped suddenly as the ivory pip turned red. "Bingo!" He said, showing her the compass before tucking it back into his jacket's inner pocket and securing it with a button. He marked the site by stepping a shovel into the damp soil. "Let's go get the excavator."

"Think it can make the ditch?"

He shrugged. "Worth trying. Otherwise we're doing this by hand in the dark, and you know what that means."

She shuddered at the thought. "I'll find the narrowest crossing."

"As long as the excavator's tread is longer than the gap, we should be fine."

As he went back to the truck, she walked the length of the ditch and found a pinched section with weed-covered soil on either side. She flagged him down and he drove the excavator her way.

As he approached the edge, he dropped the boom on the other side of the ditch, using it as a crutch to keep the treads level over the gap until the far side of the treads were back on terra firma. As the excavator straddled the ditch, he rotated the boom toward the side closest to the road and countered the weight until the entire thing was solidly on the other side. Crushing the fence was a breeze compared to that maneuver.

As with all of her colleagues, Wilson had started out a black box. There was a swath of information she didn't know about his past or skills. She knew better than to ask questions, but that didn't stop her from collecting the scraps he allowed her to know and piece together a composite. After that performance, she confidently added "proficient at operating earth moving equipment" to her mental profile of him.

It was dark by the time they returned to the planted shovel, and they worked by the light of the excavator. Since they didn't know exactly what they were looking for, they didn't know how large it would be. It could be a body, but it could also be an object, like a phylactery or a Koschei needle.

They proceeded with caution. He would deposit a bucket of soil ten feet away and she would check it with the compass. If there was no red pip in the newly upturned dirt, he kept digging. They were three feet down when the wind picked up tussling the treetops. Thick clouds rolled in from the south threatening rain, which was the last thing they needed.

As Martinez was checking the latest batch of soil, Wilson caught movement in the darkness—a cluster of shadows with thick round bodies and slender, narrow necks was seeping out of the tree line. They were behind her and coming closer. She was oblivious to them and he doubted she heard much over the noise of the excavator.

"Behind you!" he yelled. He drew his Glock and leapt down from the excavator with unnatural speed. Before Martinez could even register his warning, he was by her side and covering her back. If there weren't so many of the shadows, he would have been excited that his augmentation magic happened so reflexively.

Martinez immediately dropped the compass and drew her weapon. The flashlight in her other hand splashed light in the direction of the approaching shadows as she twisted. The beam wasn't strong enough to illuminate very far, but the boom slowly spun and cast its brighter light in that direction—in his haste, Wilson had forgotten to lock it before jumping out.

Sixty feet away, a herd of curious, black-furred alpacas fled the sudden movement and bright light. Martinez laughed out loud as she lowered her weapon. "I suppose there are worse ways to die, especially in our profession."

He chuckled. "Sure, but scared to death by alpaca is patently ridiculous."

"How do you know they aren't llamas?" she asked as she holstered her gun and secured the compass.

"Alpaca travel in herds, llamas are loners," he answered as he put his own Glock away.

"I had no idea camelids were an interest of yours," she said drily. She moved her hand toward the last dumped bucket load of dirt, "This load is clean, but I think we are getting close."

Wilson tensed up. "Do you smell something?"

"No, but I'm getting the growing urge to stop working, lie back in the soft grass and stargaze, and the only constellation I can reliably pick out is the big dipper," she replied. "It's the same thing that happened to me when I ran into a field of narcissus flowers."

He was relieved but genuinely puzzled. "Then why aren't I affected?"

"Once bitten, twice shy? You gonna talk or you gonna dig?" she nudged him back on task. If whatever was buried here was magicked not to be found, any distraction was working against them. He nodded and waited for the boom to slowly sweep back into place before climbing into the cab.

They continued their search and at the four-foot mark, the bucket scrapped against something solid. Wilson locked the boom with the lights on the gaping hole. He put on work gloves and grabbed one of the shovels, prodding along its edge to get an idea of its size and shape.

"It's big," he stated after probing a yard. "I'm going to dig a ramp on one side so we can use the shovels properly." Martinez stepped out of the way and watched the tree line, just in case there was more than curious alpacas in the darkness.

Now that he knew where the hidden object was, he could quickly clear vast amounts of ground without fear of damaging it. They stepped into the trench and started clearing the surface dirt. Underneath, it was smooth, leathery, mottled brown and shiny—a sparkle that reminded Wilson of the magic mushrooms of the fairy ring.

"It's definitely fae," he attested and knelt down for a closer look with the flashlight. "You know, it kind of looks like an egg," he observed. "Like a giant reptile egg."

Martinez shook her head—she'd seen enough science fiction movies to know eggs were bad news. "Let's dig this sucker out and get it packed in salt before it has a chance to hatch."

She drew her weapon while he worked around the edges, loosening the perimeter to guide the excavator's next bucket load. If whatever was inside attacked, one bullet should be enough to send it back to the Land of Fae.

Eventually, they found its full length was six feet and its shape was more cylindrical than egg-shaped. The form and angles were also all wrong and it took Martinez a second to figure out why it looked so familiar. "That's not an egg," she said emphatically. "It's a chrysalis."

Chapter Eighteen

Detroit, Michigan, USA
11th of March, 9:10 a.m. (GMT-5)

Wilson woke as the roar of the road noise suddenly quieted. Martinez was bringing the truck to a stop at exit 45 on I-75. "How long have I been out?" he asked groggily. "Last I remember was Saginaw."

"About two hours," she answered, taking a left turn that would lead to the last mile of their very long road trip. It had taken several hours to fully unearth the chrysalis, back fill the gaping hole, and repack the box truck. It was nearly midnight when they left Manitoulin Island and it was a unanimous decision to press on, driving through the night in shifts instead of staying the night somewhere. The sooner the chrysalis was safely in the Mine, the better.

They'd phoned in their ETA a few hours ago and LaSalle had laid the groundwork for their return. They approached the gate for freight deliveries and passed their doctored paperwork to the guard. He was expecting them and waved them through without much scrutiny.

Martinez had never used the freight elevator and was glad

to finally get to see it in action. As soon as they cleared the platform, the gates closed behind them and she killed the engine. She followed the training protocol, holding her hands up in plain sight and confirmed her identity at the scanners after him. When they both got the green light, LaSalle entered, except there were no armed men to stand down.

"Welcome back," LaSalle greeted them. "Any difficulties along the way?" Wilson noted his question was directed at Martinez.

She shook her head. "Nope. Everything went smoothly except for a brief alpaca scare." Wilson stopped himself from smiling as he noted the playful familiarity in her answer.

"Good. I'm going to need your help getting it unloaded." LaSalle approached the scanner and the platform started its descent.

"I noticed the lack of security," Wilson posited an inquiry with a statement of fact.

"Leader wants to keep a lid on this," LaSalle explained as he readied for the first stop. He scanned his eye and palm but pressed a different code into the keypad. They weren't stopping at interrogation this time. They were going deeper.

In addition to quarantine of unknown magical objects, the freight elevator was also used to transport those that were identified but too large to fit in the passenger elevator. Even though none of them knew what their package was, it was obvious that Leader did and that was enough to bypass the security protocol.

The light from the bottom of the shaft slowly grew brighter as they descended into a secure storage area well below the library. The massive cavern was huge, at least eight times the length of the repository and more than three times its height. Along the wing, a series a four docks backed up to four eldritch doors of silver and gold.

Martinez got out and guided Wilson to the right dock while LaSalle opened the door and got the forklift. By the time Wilson had the box truck backed into dock C, LaSalle was ready to receive the package.

Wilson moved the mini-excavator while Martinez showed LaSalle the large container that held the chrysalis. Once LaSalle had the payload, he wheeled it into the long corridor and bid them to follow. Once everyone was inside, the tall man closed the door behind them.

"Climb aboard—we're at the end of the hall," he instructed them.

"Who's we?" Wilson asked as he grabbed onto one side of the forklift and Martinez the other.

"Leader, Chloe and Dot," he responded before taking off. The high-pitched whine of the electric engine prohibited any more conversation as they passed through spurts of dim industrial lighting in the otherwise dark tunnel. Each light coincided with a sigil-etched door, most of which were the size of a single garage door. This was new territory for both agents, and Wilson wondered if they were going to the end because the other rooms were full or because Leader wanted the package as far away from the way out as possible.

After a mile of travel, LaSalle brought the forklift to a stop before a doublewide sigiled door. The agents hopped off and he opened the door into a long rectangular room revealing the waiting forms of Chloe and Dot, and Leader. The interior was scantly furnished: a dual-bulb industrial work lamp, a few aluminum-framed lawn chairs that were at least as old as Wilson by the look of their plaid plastic webbing, and a cot holding an unconscious Megan Anderson.

"Finally!" Dot exclaimed as they entered and LaSalle returned to the forklift to drive the container inside.

It was Leader who shut the door behind them. "All right," she said, switching on the bright lights. "Let's see what we're dealing with."

LaSalle set the container down in front of the floodlights and Wilson and Martinez popped the lid. They carefully pushed away the salt on the top, revealing the chitinous chrysalis. It was scintillating in the full light and looked much less leathery than when they'd loaded it. The twins and Leader ran their individual wills over the exposed surface before looking at one another.

"Any concerns?" Leader gave the sisters a chance to voice dissent.

"None," Chloe and Dot responded in unison.

"Fulcrum, Lancer, please get it out of the container and put it on the ground. David, if you would move the light directly behind it, we should be able to get some idea of what's inside," Leader ordered.

Wilson and Martinez found wrangling it out of the container much easier than putting it in. Salt scattered across the floor as they tipped the container on its side and rolled the chrysalis out. It was warmer to the touch than before, but that was hardly surprising. It must have been close to freezing that deep in the Canadian ground.

LaSalle picked up the heavy lamp with ease, pulling on the cord for the extra slack he needed. He turned it upside down and positioned the bulbs. The concentrated light revealed a slim form inside; the silhouette's curves and gross anatomy suggested it was a female human. "Is that the body of whatever is inside Anderson?" he asked.

Leader didn't speak but answered with a curt nod. "You've both done well," she addressed her agents. "You must be exhausted after driving through the night. Go home and get some rest. Fulcrum, before you leave, pinpoint the exact coordinates of the fairy ring you dismantled with David." Wilson wanted to know more about what was happening, but the thought of his own bed was suddenly very appealing.

Then Leader turned to LaSalle. "David, if you'd escort Lancer and Fulcrum to the surface with the box truck, we'll get to work down here. We should be done by the time you return."

The rigidity in his jaw suggested he wasn't entirely pleased with the situation. He was Leader's personal security, and if he didn't know what the chrysalis was or what it was capable of he couldn't perform to his full capacity. Nonetheless, he righted the lamp before setting it down and complied with her wishes.

Once the agents had left with LaSalle and the sigiled door was shut, Chloe and Dot giggled like schoolgirls. "I can't believe it's here!" Chloe clapped in delight. Even Dot squealed.

Leader dropped her neutral facade and smiled. She ran her hands over the chrysalis and it hummed under her touch. "After all this time," she said reverently.

They dragged the cot beside the sparkling chamber and prepared for the ritual at hand. The three women linked hands and wills and spun ribbons of magic around Megan Anderson until she was completely encased. Then they pressed the cocoon made of their metaphysical silk to the chrysalis and spoke their collective will. The hardened shell that had spent centuries in the moist earth of Manitoulin Island magically softened. The chitinous shell roiled as it absorbed the body of Megan Anderson, giving off incredible heat in the intake. Soon the process they had begun was past the point of no return, but under their skill the melding was safely completed. All that remained was a singular chrysalis slightly fuller than before.

"Is that it?" Dot wondered out loud when they were finished. She didn't *exactly* know what was going to happen but a hot and plump chrysalis was rather anticlimactic.

"Give it time to work," Chloe chided her sister. "You can't rush these things. Right, Pen?"

Leader put her hand on the surface and felt the churning underneath the still shell. It was breaking down what once was in order to transform into what it would become. "Don't worry. It's cooking."

Chapter Nineteen

Sumpter Township, Michigan, USA
12th of March, 11:40 a.m. (GMT-5)

LaSalle parked the bulletproof and magically warded SUV in the graveled driveway of the farm. The winter crops had yet to be turned under, and the greenhouse was filled with flats waiting to grow into seedlings to be planted after the last frost. In addition to fresh produce, the farm—owned by a shell corporation of Discretion Minerals—provided Salt Mine agents a secluded place to enter the Magh Meall.

"We're here," he announced. Seated in the back, Leader was dressed in natural earth tone fabrics and there wasn't any metal in her attire. If he had any doubts about her intention, the trenching tool, packed lunch, and box of shortbread quelled them. He'd worked for Leader for a long time, but she'd never asked him to drive her to the farm until today.

"Wait here. It shouldn't take more than an hour. If the Mine or one of the agents needs you, feel free to leave. I'll find my way back. If I'm gone for more than eight hours, notify Chloe and Dot. They'll know what to do," she instructed her faithful assistant-slash-bodyguard. He acknowledged the order even though he would have preferred to accompany her. When he'd offered, she firmly declined. She even insisted on trenching the circle herself.

He watched her climb out of the vehicle and enter the wooded area with her gear. Once she was out of sight, he repositioned the SUV to face the path so he could immediately see her when she exited the woods. He cracked the window before turning off the engine and pulled out his tablet.

Leader ventured deeper and found a clearing among the shadows of the surrounding trees. She went through the motions even though they were not necessary. She dug a tight circle with the shovel, crumbled a line of shortbread around the perimeter, and placed four lit candles at the cardinal directions. Everything would look as it should if anyone were to stumble onto the site. Optics were everything

Then, she paused for lunch: an egg salad sandwich and a few cookies that were not used in preparing the circle, washed down with water from her waterskin. She took off her watch—the only piece of metal on her person—and placed it on top of her bag outside of the circle. When the hands ticked over to twelve, she closed her eyes and formed a golden sphere of her will in the palm of her hand. She focused on the precise coordinates Fulcrum had identified with LaSalle on the military satellite photos. Once it was fixed in her mind, she inflated the sphere in her hand until it entirely encased her,

When the sweet smell of the Magh Meall filled her nostrils,

she popped the bubble. As soon as she made contact with the ground, she drank deep of the ancient power that rushed through the earth beneath her feet. She opened her eyes and immediately looked up at the massive trees towering above her. If she were very quiet, she could hear them breathe. She found herself smiling. It had been a long time since she'd visited the middle lands and was pleasantly surprised to find it lived up to her memory of the place.

Reluctantly, she reined in her wonder. As much as she longed to reconnect to the mystic rhythms around her, she had a job to do. If all went well, she could always take the long route back.

She surveyed the ground and stopped when she found the remains of the defunct fairy ring bathed in purple-tinged sunlight. A few mushrooms had popped up since Fulcrum's efforts, but the ring remained unpowered. Knowing the curiosity of the fae, she approached and admired the tenacious buds.

After five minutes, she felt a pair of inquisitive eyes upon her. Without moving, Leader spoke gently. "You can come out. I'm not going to hurt you."

From the tree line, a barky feminine face peaked out from behind a thick trunk. Timidly, the rest of the hamadryad followed suit and she curtsied, lowering her head until it was well below Leader's five foot height. "My apologies. I did not mean to offend," she spoke ingratiatingly.

"You have caused no offense," Leader replied. "Are you the one who met a human maker here not too long ago?"

The dryad's shoulders tightened. "I treated him fairly," she answered defensively.

"That is an opinion he shares," she reassured her. "He said he made some gifts for you in exchange for your assistance."

The dryad's silky green hair shimmered in the light as she nodded. "He did," she confirmed.

"Good. Come here, I would like to see them." There was no magic in Leader's words, but the fae found herself stepping forward without hesitation or thought. Once the first step was taken, she did not think it wise to not take the others.

With every step, she humbled herself lower to the ground in an effort to make herself small. When she came to Leader's feet, she summoned the six vibrant mushrooms from her chest and offered them with extended hands.

Leader picked up one by one and appraised them in the light. Considering they were made under pressure and without preparation, they weren't bad. Fulcrum was growing; not long ago, it would have been beyond his skills.

On the final one, she quickly spun a line of her will, matching his esoteric pattern, and tied it off. "Pretty gifts for a pretty creature," she complimented the dryad as she returned the altered vermillion mushroom. The flattered fae placed all of them back into her chest and took a step back.

"I have added something to the red one," Leader stated

plainly.

The hamadryad's skin began to grow spikes as involuntary spasms of fear ran through her—she had inadvertently accepted a gift without making a bargain first!

"Do not worry, little one," Leader spoke in a calm lilt. "I have simply made it last as long as I will. That one will not fade when the previous maker perishes."

The dryad brought her skin under control and held herself with the poise and grace befitting one of her kind. "What a kind gift. And what would you have me do in return?"

Leader was amused at her pluck and courage. "All I ask is that you carry me to the cave entrance you showed the other maker and that you never speak of our encounter."

The weight in the dryad's chest lightened and she bowed. "Of course," she said as she touched her will lightly against Leader's. The spark was electrifying.

The dryad grew taller to accommodate Leader. When the petite woman was safely cradled in her arms, she grew to her full height and flew through the forest, changing the length of her legs as the terrain varied to keep the ride smooth for her passenger.

When they reached the drop off, the dryad's feet grew roots and tendrils that grasped the cliff face, and the fae scaled them with the same ease as walking on the soft forest soil. She gently placed Leader down in front of the cave entrance and bowed again before retreating into the woods of the valley.

Leader waited until the hamadryad was well out of range before approaching the cave. Her will glossed over the wards placed on the interior lip of the dark mouth. When she found nothing unexpected, she smashed them all before entering. The purple-tinged light of the Magh Meall traveled farther into the gloomy depths than the white light of Sol would have, but eventually it too faded, so she ensorcelled her eyes to see in the permanent darkness under the surface of the middle lands.

The caves looked similar to those of the mortal realm, replete with stalactites, stalagmites, and formations of such ilk, even if their generative force differed from Earth. Here, they were sculpted out of the will of their inhabitants instead of erosion and geological forces. It was arguable who was mimicking whom, but the concurrence was undeniable.

She hadn't traveled very deep before she heard movement and retreated to a defensible location that gave her a long vantage point. In the quiet, she counted the steps to get an idea of what was coming her way: a full-sized expulsion party of Dökkálfar.

Good, they heard my knock, she thought as she waited for the inevitable scouts to round the bend. It was the dark elves' standard tactic to send a pair of scouts ahead of the main force; even if one was taken down, the second could retreat and warn the others.

The duo paused when they caught sight of Leader and she stayed perfectly still, pretending not to be able to see the glamoured scouts. While some fae could bend light to render themselves effectively invisible, the Dökkálfar had learned to bend the darkness to much the same effect. Like all of their kind, they had pale pasty skin and long white hair tied back for combat. They were dressed in traditionally hardened cuir bouilli that had inspired the Ancient Greeks' and Romans' armor.

They exchanged some quick words via sign language, and one silently descended into the curving depths while the other remained behind. When the approaching scout was within twenty feet, Leader shattered its glamour and addressed it. "I seek audience with your leader."

Unexpectedly revealed in front of her, it drew its crystalline dagger while the one in the back sprung into motion and disappeared from sight. Leader expected no less and her statement was actually for the retreating scout. She put her attacker to sleep with a wave of her will and tucked the body into a depression behind one of the decorative stalagmites. She took her original position and waited for the oncoming platoon.

She recognized the second scout as it rounded the corner. "I have no wish to harm you. I simply need to speak to your leader," she spoke as soon as she saw it.

"Then, speak," a commanding voice boomed, followed by its equally proud form. Its face and torso was solidly Dökkálfar, but its back half was thirty feet of giant centipede ending with a stinger: a centiturion. Only the most powerful among the dark elves could twist the magic of their curse through ritual and sacrifice to take such shape. "I am here. Speak your peace and be gone!"

The rest of the squad filed in behind the centiturion: foot soldiers with spears and archers armed with bent mushroom and bone shortbows. She scanned them as a whole: they were determined and serious in the face of a threat.

Unmoved by its attempt at intimidation, Leader corrected the centiturion. "You may be leader of this band, but I wish to speak to Mikillævi." The soldiers whispered to each other at the mention of the clan's matriarch, but they quieted with a flap of the centiturion's venomous tail.

"Impossible! Go now or we shall kill you for the murder of our comrade," the centiturion threatened. It tried to project authority but Leader heard the fear in its voice. Fear made all creatures do stupid things. If the centiturion couldn't be reasoned with, this was going to take longer than it needed.

"It is not dead. You will find it behind me, asleep against the stone," she responded and stepped back, giving it wide berth. "You can check for yourself if you don't believe me." The centiturion motioned for a pair of veteran soldiers to retrieve the body.

Once they had the slumbering scout behind their ranks, she spoke, "You have found me true to my word. Again, I seek audience with Mikillævi and my patience grows thin. I do not want to unravel the nodes of travel alone, but I will do so if you fail to escort me." She deliberately left out what their fate would be if they choose that path.

"How do you know of the nodes?" the fae questioned.

"I am a knower of things," she answered curtly.

The nodes linking the various Dökkálfar outposts to their mother cities were a closely guarded secret and were unrecognizable from the normal veins of quartz found everywhere in the rocks of the Magh Meall. Her knowledge of them clearly rattled both the centiturion and its troops.

One of the soldiers broke discipline and yelled, "It has no weapons, just slay it!" The cry brought murmurs of agreement from the other soldiers, and the centiturion flicked its tail to regain order. Despite this, an arrow was loosed and its aim was true. It flew straight for Leader's chest.

She plucked it out of the air and looked it over. It was made of ash, and tipped with magical crystal. "Nice craftsmanship," she commented before dropping it. "You grossly misunderstand the situation. I *am* going to see Mikillævi and she will gift me her endless favor after our meeting. You are standing not just in my way, but in *hers*."

Chapter Twenty

The Land of Fae

Once upon a time in a land far, far away, there was an enchanted world filled with magical beings. Comely in appearance yet capricious in spirit, they came to be known as faeries and their home the Land of Fae. In the center of the land was an eld place called Tír na nÓg, where the imperial palace lay, and from whence Oberon and Titania dispensed justice. They were the last two of the Fomoire, the ancient progenitor race from which all fae descended.

Around them was the council of seven fae clans of royal blood, known as the Tuatha Dé Danann, who saw to the administration of the realm. All were achingly beautiful but varied in appearance as each house sought to distinguish itself from the other, as only the grand fae were able to choose their appearance. Members of House Sarvahna had hazelnut skin and inquisitive malachite eyes, while House Mimallones favored olive skin and piercing hematite orbs. House Dela was fair skinned with sparkling emerald irises and they always dressed in royal gold and blue to set themselves apart from House Bereginyas, who shared coloring except that they preferred hair of sable.

In his infinite wisdom, Oberon had carved out Tír na nÓg as the special place for the royal houses so he could keep a close watch over his prideful spawn, but no matter how vast he made the land, it never was large enough to hold in peace all seven houses nor calm their grudges. Locked in an endless cycle of insult and retaliation, their conflicts cascaded into other realms, played out by and through their vessels and agents. Never were there direct assaults, but that didn't lessen their turmoil, it merely swept the conflict into the darkness and out of sight.

And then unexpectedly there was a blessed birth. While countless faeries came into being in every epoch, it had been ages since a new Fomoir had been conceived. The offspring of Oberon and Titania was celebrated throughout the entire realm and into neighboring ones. Its cry was more lyrical than the nightingale's song, its laughter more refreshing than a cool breeze on a hot summer's day, and its silver eyes sparkled brighter than any star in the night sky.

For a moment, faeries high and low ceased their machinations and petty grievances. Titania had high hopes that her child could spur a new age of peace. The Fomoire were the very soul of the fae, and the birth of a new one was proof that their kind was fecund, not dying on the vine as so many worried.

To herald the occasion, Oberon threw a lavish party and opened the imperial palace to all the Tuatha Dé Danann. He too hoped new life could heal old wounds. All the birds in the realms sang sweet songs and the flowers offered their blooms to make the endless garlands. Mountains of ambrosia and rivers of nectar were gathered for the feast. Even the fae that dwelt in the middle lands, in the purple-tinged Magh Meall, were invited home for the festivities, although the imperial palace remained off limits to their weaker seed.

But amidst the cheery bustle, dark intent found its opening and tragedy struck at the imperial heart—the child of Titania and Oberon was abducted! They scoured the land but found no trace of their progeny. Wherever their child was, it was outside of their vision and sphere of power. Titania's tears filled the oceans and Oberon's rage was felt across all the land. It was so great that even the rocks boiled in the mortal realms.

The Land of Fae was struck dumb by the egregious act and all the royal houses voiced their outrage while denying involvement. They were quick to lay the blame on some strange intruder, an unnamed and faceless Other who must have snuck into the fair realm, but Oberon was not convinced by their pretty words. Only they had entrance to the imperial palace and even in his great grief, he could sense the sin somewhere among their hearts—were they not also the fruit of his proverbial loins?

He demanded satisfaction and when guilt was finally determined, it fell on House Bereginyas. The hammer of his justice was hard and swift now that it had a target. Oberon stripped the entire house of their name and cursed them to no longer feel the warmth and light of the sun in any realm. As he spoke his will into power, their silky ebon locks drained of color and their milky skin turned pasty. Their emerald eyes became solid black and angular, like pieces of faceted black tourmaline. Their soft, colorful silks were torn from their bodies and they were cast out of the Land of Fae. Thus, the Dökkálfar were born.

The remaining six houses were stunned at the severity of the decree but none dared challenge it. Instead, they inquired about the seventh seat on the council. There could be no question of leaving it empty; there had to be an odd number lest nothing be decided. And that was when Titania spoke, declaring to the realms that the only thing more terrible than the rage of a father was the sorrow of a mother. She swore to reward whoever destroyed the Dökkálfar with the highest of honors: the lesser house that eradicated them would gain their place among the Tuatha Dé Danann, but none of the royal houses were allowed to influence the contest.

And then Oberon and Titania together forged their final edict: those that knew of this great injustice would never forget it, but their tongues were forever sealed and never could they speak of it. All of Fae felt their will ripple out and none were spared. They were all cursed with solitary and silent remembrance.

Chapter Twenty-One

Sumpter Township, Michigan, USA
13th of March, 11:30 p.m. (GMT-5)

"Careful!" Chloe scolded Wilson as he took one end of the chrysalis in hand with LaSalle on the other.

"I am being careful," he replied between clenched teeth and fixed his grip again. It never had handholds, but it was significantly harder to grasp now that it was heavier, fatter, and slippery. Whatever Leader and the librarians had done to it, it was slick like a waxy tree leaf and completely iridescent.

Wilson was strong for his size, but at five-foot-five, he didn't have LaSalle's ridiculous arm span. He nodded when he was ready for another go and scrambled to get underneath it as the hulk of a man on the other end effortlessly lifted.

With the twins' directions, the men managed to ease the chrysalis out of Leader's SUV onto the sled attached to the back of a four-wheeler. Wilson tied it down with straps while the twins closed the SUV and LaSalle climbed into the driver's seat of the four-wheeler. The engine roared and he drove slowly, taking exceptional care with the load.

It wasn't long until they reached the small clearing where

Leader was trenching a circle large enough to contain the chrysalis. Wilson had never seen her do manual labor before; the efficiency in her movement suggested this wasn't her first time with a shovel. She, like Wilson, was dressed for the Magh Meall but LaSalle and Chloe and Dot were not.

It was a contention discussion that boiled down to two incontrovertible facts: Leader had to go and if things went sideways, the Salt Mine would need LaSalle and the librarians. Wilson wasn't sure what was going on, but even Chloe looked pissed and Dot had an expression he'd long ago learned to avoid.

He and LaSalle unloaded the chrysalis and arranged it on the north-south axis. After it was in position, Wilson finished the circle with crushed shortbread and lit candles. By the time he'd finished, LaSalle, Chloe, and Dot had taken their leave.

Leader pulled a belt and sword from a bag that was too small to have held it. "Take this. Don't draw it unless you absolutely must, and if you do, show no mercy." Her gray eyes were deadly serious.

Wilson took it in hand and examined the anti-summoning wards on the blade—it was uncannily similar to the arming sword Moncrief had given him when they'd faced down Morc mac Dela. "This is one of the Vlfberhts, isn't it?"

"Yes," she answered tersely while she strapped on her own weapon. Were he with Moncrief, he would have asked about it, but refrained since it was Leader. If he needed to know about her sword, she would tell him.

"Did you eat?" she inquired.

"In the car on the way over," he affirmed

"Then let's start," she said as she sat cross-legged on one side of the chrysalis and motioned for him to sit on the other side. "I'll get us there; you focus your will on protecting this from harm."

Wilson nodded, a little disappointed that the prospect of entering into ritual with Leader was taken off the table. He would have loved to take a peek at her esoteric work.

Leader wrapped her will around them like building a ball of twine. She could have gone the fast way but chose a more established route of travel since they were carrying precious cargo. After a few layers, she felt the circle shift and change direction. Wilson involuntarily cried out as he felt the ground underneath him give way. The chrysalis was pulling their ball where it wanted to go, and it was going fast.

"Remain calm!" she ordered as they plummeted toward the Magh Meall. She didn't try to regain control and instead planted her arm atop the chrysalis. "Do not speak unless spoken to, Fulcrum. Whatever happens, your job is to protect whatever comes out of this."

It felt like the freefall of skydiving, only he didn't have a parachute. Leader changed the shape of her will to a bubble to cushion the landing. When they came to a crashing halt, the bubble burst from the impact, but those within the circle were unharmed, chrysalis included.

They had landed on a mesa overlooking a massive plain that stretched as far as the eye could see. He knew they were in the Magh Meall—the light was tinted purple and the air impossibly clean and sweet—but there wasn't a tree in sight. Where in the world was a place so holy that the middle land's counterpoint would be so utterly devoid of trees? And more importantly, how did they get there?

He turned to Leader for answers. "What happened?"

"Be quiet!" she snapped. She was never one to mince words, but there was actual emotion in her voice. He didn't know what to do with that. He watched Leader run her hands over the chrysalis as she examined it. He wanted to ask what she saw that he could not but went mute when he saw her smile—a broad, unabashed grin. Her joy was so pure, he forgot for a moment that this was the same person who could stop a charging rhino with just a sharp look.

Then, he saw something move inside the chrysalis. The iridescent shell bulged as something pressed from the inside. Suddenly, a crack appeared and the subsequent release of energy knocked Wilson back. The shockwave rippled out and he regained his feet in time to see it cross the expanse.

As it traveled, he became one with it and his own vision increased. Miles became hundreds of miles, to thousands, to hundreds of thousands—all taken in with a single glance. His head reeled and he fell to his knees, struggling to master his ever-expanding view. Behind him, he heard another series of cracks, followed by Leader's gleeful giggles. That's when he sensed they were no longer alone.

"I am, at last!" declared a voice so unique, it was beauty itself coupled with an immense power that would eclipse the puissant might of Poseidon himself. Wilson turned his head and saw the chrysalis split wide open. He immediately recognized Megan Anderson's unconscious form covered in slime beside the now-empty shell. Standing on the other side was a figure obscured by bright light.

It was like staring at the sun, only brighter. He immediately looked away but the image was burned into his retinas and he could still see the large butterfly wings even though his eyes were shut. He could feel his life force burning away in proximity of the intense power. Bits of his soul drifted away in a trail of sooty smoke that turned into golden dust as it danced over the mesa.

Remembering Leader's final order, he summon his will *Think...think...think...* Eyes clamped shut, he crawled toward Megan's body. If he could reach her before he was consumed by the fiery light, he could jettison them out of the Magh Meall and back into the mortal realm. Wherever the corollary on Earth, it had to be safer than their current predicament.

The crushing energy suddenly eased, and Wilson gasped like a swimmer coming up from a deep dive. The same lyrical voice spoke again, "Forgive me, champion, I forget the power of my true form."

He opened his eyes again; the figure was terrible, but no longer lethal. The magnificent butterfly wings were holding aloft a faerie of such indescribable loveliness that there simply weren't words. She was the epitome of Fae in its platonic form. For every aspect of her that he could perceive, he knew there were multitudes outside of his comprehension but he felt them in his soul nonetheless.

"Take care of this one when you return her to your realm," she said as she cleaned the slime from Anderson's body with a sweep of her hand. "She is good of heart and an unwitting jailor." Wilson was so stunned by her presence that he could say nothing and showed his understanding by placing a protective hand on Anderson's warm shoulder. He would never be the same for the viewing.

The Fae turned her attention to Leader, "Are you master of this servant, blooded one?"

Leader graciously dropped into a curtsy and lowered her grey eyes in respect. "I am."

"Then we are in your debt," she pronounced. As she uttered the final syllable, the entire realm resonated, like the chime of a struck bell. All creatures within the land stood witness—Alberia, the daughter of Oberon and Titania was in the middle lands, and she had made an obligation.

Alberia flew over the edge of the mesa, raised her hands, and unleashed her power, but this time, she consciously shielded Wilson and Anderson from her magnificence. Thick black clouds appeared, blocking out the purple-tinged light. "Come to me, Dökkálfar!" she commanded.

Throughout Wilson's hyperextended vision, mounds of dirt were disturbed as all the Dökkálfar were pulled out of the ground, like moles drawn out of their holes. They writhed in the dim light and those that were powerful enough threw up shields, allowing them to temporarily stand the killing light. Those less fortunate started to smoke despite the thick cloud cover.

Alberia spoke her will. "You who were punished for violence against those who breathed life into your dull form, fear not the warmth and light of the sun. You are absolved of guilt, for you were never guilty. Be restored, noble House Bereginyas!"

She waved her hand and the cursed and twisted forms of the Dökkálfar were transformed into their original radiant bodies. Gone were the pasty skin and white hair, replaced by the alabaster and sable. Hard obsidian eyes sparkled emerald once again. And most importantly, their primitive clothing—the boiled hides of beasts—had vanished and in their place were diaphanous silks and satins befitting their royal station.

Alberia turned her head to the west and a rainbow appeared, filling the entire western sky. Wilson had never seen a truer rainbow. Beyond the bands of color, he could see into Fae itself, even into fabled Tír na nÓg where no mortal had ever visited. Had Alberia not shielded him, he would have faded before its glory.

"Your true home awaits you," she declared. A great cry of joy arose from the Magh Meall as countless members of House Bereginyas took to the air and swarmed the rainbow, basking in the light they had long been denied.

Only the lowliest of the clan remained on the ground, servants unable to join their masters in flight. To them, Alberia bestowed her next decree. "To you who bore a crueler fate than your winged brethren could know, be transformed. May those who have suffered together fly together." Delicate wings sprouted from the backs of billions of tiny fae, and they too rose into the sky, triumphantly flying to their ancestral home.

On the far side of the rainbow, two luminous figures suddenly appeared and the mass of House Bereginyas moved aside to make way for their approach. Like Alberia, they were beyond any words Wilson knew, and even with her protection, he had to look away—there were only so many Fomoire the human eye could hold at once.

"Alberia? Is it really you?" Titania spoke in disbelief.

"Where have you been all this time, sweet child?" Oberon said in that sternness that sprung from worry and love.

Alberia smiled at the sight of her parents and the Magh Meall felt its radiant warmth. "I was split in twain and trapped in a mortal cage life after life after life, but I have returned. I am here to right wrongs, for it wasn't House Bereginyas that wronged us."

"Who then? Oberon demanded. "Speak their name and let them stand judgment."

"Father, it is my justice to dispense," she insisted.

Titania and Oberon exchanged a look and came to a silent consensus. "So be it, Alberia."

Her sweet disposition turned to fury. "Come to me, House Dela, House Tantali!" she commanded. In an instant, their multitude were pulled into the Magh Meall and filled the endless plain. "The judgment of my esteemed mother and father stands, but to theirs I add my own. Since you were joined in your evil, you will now be joined in blood. Neither will have royal blood flow through their clan."

In his preternatural gaze, Wilson saw the erasure of House Dela and House Tantali occur in real time. It was like watching someone mix all the primary colors of paint until it was a lump of homogenous brown.

"You are now the Dökkálfar and subject to the fate that was decreed to them all those ages ago. May the lesser house that eradicates you join the pride of Tír na nÓg," Alberia pronounced. As she spoke the words, countless iridescent wings fell from shoulders and beauty faded into foulness.

And then she raised her hands to the sky and the clouds parted. Those Dökkálfar who were too slow in their retreat underground perished in the purple light of the Magh Meall. Titania and Oberon beamed at their offspring. She had grown much in her absence and was no longer a child.

Epilogue

Marshall, Michigan, USA
13th of March, 5:55 p.m. (GMT-5)

Megan Anderson stirred softly as she roused. She had a bad case of cottonmouth and her head was killing her. *Was I drugged?* she wondered as her consciousness slowly came back online. She followed the breadcrumbs of memory: Darren in the cafe, going to her parent's hunting cottage, the armed man that broke in and then protected her, and then shit got really weird.

She fully woke when a male voice spoke over the road noise. "There's a bottle of water in the cup holder. It will help the headache."

The late afternoon sunlight smarted as she opened her eyes. She had no idea where they were, but they were driving on a highway. She kicked herself—how many times had her dad told her: always drive yourself.

She stifled the rising panic and took stock of her situation. She was seated in the passenger seat, unbound but belted in. She recognized the driver as the same FBI agent from before, except the last thing she remembered was pulling up for a giant monster garage door in the dark.

"Where are we?" she croaked as she reached for the bottle of water. She checked for signs of tampering but the plastic seal was still intact and a gentle squeeze revealed no puncture holes.

Wilson noted her caution in his periphery—once bitten, twice shy. "We're fifteen minutes from your parent's house," he answered as he steered his British racing green Porsche 911 west on I-94.

She broke the seal with a firm twist. "What happened and why do I feel like I have the worse hangover ever?" The cool water running down her throat was like manna from heaven.

"You've been unconscious for the past four days, but in that time, I've managed to get some answers and fix things," he answered succinctly.

With her thirst slaked, her brain fired up. She immediately gave herself a five-point inspection—nothing hurt except for her head and the water *did* help. "Am I still being chased?"

"No, the FBI has taken the case over," he informed her.

"And the faeries?" she inquired.

"The thing they were looking for was hidden inside of you, but we were able to remove it safely. That's why you had to be kept unconscious. If you were awake, you probably wouldn't have survived the procedure," he explained things in layman's terms.

"Like putting someone under before surgery?" she took a stab in the dark.

He subtly moved his head side to side. "Something like that."

"What did you take out of me?" she questioned him.

He heard anxiety in her voice and did his best to reassure her while keeping his eyes on the road. "Something that shouldn't have been there in the first place, but we only took out what didn't belong."

"We?" she followed up, glomming onto the plural.

"The organization I work for," he answered with a firm full stop.

She didn't have the energy to run headlong against that wall and skirted around it. "And all that stuff about magic?"

"It's still true, but you don't have to worry about that anymore. No more rainbows shooting out of your hand." The memory of Alberia's rainbow flashed in his mind's eye.

"And you're not going to wipe my memory?" she asked suspiciously.

He smirked. "You've been watching too many movies." He elided over the truth—she'd be dead if her silence was mission critical, but Alberia ensured her former host remained ignorant of her presence. "You are no longer capable of hurting people with magic and if you tried to tell anyone what happened, it's just too unbelievable. It's not like you could reproduce the proof."

Anderson's momentary relief was quickly cut short. "What about Darren?" she said in a panic.

Wilson finally revealed the truth to her. "None of the witness at the Hummingbird Grill remembered what happened. The official report will be that the man who killed Darren abducted you, but we tracked him down and he was killed in the recovery operation. I have a few i's to dot and t's to cross, but for you, the case is closed."

Her mind replayed the events that followed. "What about my car and the money I took from my parent's safe?"

"Never happened," he confidently swept her worries aside. "Both have been returned with none the wiser."

"So it's done," she said reluctantly. It seemed too good to be true. "And I'm just supposed to pretend like it didn't happen?"

"It would be wise for you to move on and leave this in the past," he advised. "The important thing is that you know it really happened and that you're not crazy."

A flood of emotions washed over her. She was too tired to be overjoyed, but she was glad. It was finally over and she wasn't going to jail or the loony bin. But there was also an underlying sadness. "I don't want you to think I'm not grateful, but I feel weird—like I'm me, but part of me is missing at the same time. Does that make any sense?"

Wilson nodded. He completely understood. His stone face softened as he fed a dollop of will into his words. "It will take you time to get used to it, but you are still you. I promise."

Megan sat back in her seat. She was certain he wasn't telling her the *entire* truth, but she believed wholeheartedly that it was the truth.

He pulled into the long driveway of her parents' farm and parked in front of the house. He was about to exit and retrieve her things from the trunk when she stopped him. "How do I get a hold of you? In case something weird happens again."

"It won't," he stated as fact.

"Fine, in case I need to talk to someone who knows I'm not crazy," she pressed. "Like you said, who else would believe me?" She looked up and her silver eyes pleaded for a lifeline.

Wilson wanted to tell her no—that he was the last person anyone should to turn to for emotional support—but Alberia had instructed him to take care of her. He handed her a blank card with just a number. "Memorize it and burn it. Leave your name when you call and the message will get to me."

She tucked it into her bra and climbed out of the car. That was when the front door burst open. "Megan!"

A burly man a few inches over six feet crossed the gravel with his long stride. "Dad!" she answered and ran straight for his arms. He held her tight.

When he let go, Megan's mother checked her over, not unlike how a woman counts her newborn's fingers and toes. She touched Megan's face and tucked one of her daughter's honey blonde locks behind her ear. "Are you okay, sweetie?"

"Yeah, mom. Thanks to him," Megan answered and motioned to Wilson who was taking his time with luggage to give them time to greet each other.

The older woman gave him a weary smile. "Thank you for bringing her home, Agent Wilson."

"Not a problem, Mrs. Anderson," he answered with polite professionalism. "Megan has been through a lot and I wanted to make sure she got home safe and sound."

Mr. Anderson hugged his wife and his daughter and kissed them both on top of their heads. "Go on with your mother. I'll bring in your things. I want to have a word with Agent Wilson."

They stood man to man in the driveway and Mr. Anderson waited until his girls were back in the house before speaking. His voice was raw and direct. "Did he hurt her?"

"No," Wilson answered. "We got to her in time." The knot of dread and anger unraveled from the bear of a man. "But it will take some time for her to recover from the ordeal. There may be gaps in memory, strange dreams, and just feeling a little lost. Having the support of friends and family during a time like this helps a lot."

"Thanks for your help. We're grateful," he said as he grabbed Megan's things. "I can't say I'm sorry you killed the sonofabitch, but bless him for taking Darren with him before you got him." With that, Mr. Anderson entered the house and closed the door behind him.

Wilson returned to his car and loosened his tie before pulling back onto the highway. He zoned out on the drive back. Every part of him was fried and he didn't have the energy to try to pick apart everything that had happened. Usually at the end of a case he had answers, but this time he had more questions than when he started.

He took the exit for the 500 instead of Zug Island. There would be time enough write reports and request reimbursements, but tonight, he just wanted to take a shower and sleep.

As he turned the corner to his place, he saw a familiar black SUV with tinted windows parked across the street from the 500. *That's odd*, he thought as he checked his phone for missed messages. When he found none, he pulled alongside it and stopped when his window was opposite the back seat's window.

The windows rolled down and Leader spoke first. "Any problems with Ms. Anderson?" Any trace of levity or laughter he'd seen from her earlier today was gone.

"No," he answered. "She's back with her parents and I think she's smart enough to play dumb."

"Good." She passed him a slip of paper. "This is for you. It's someone you can talk to in full confidence."

Wilson unfolded it and found a name and number in her neat cursive. He'd been through psych evaluations in the CIA but it wasn't protocol in the Salt Mine. "Is this mandatory?"

"No, completely voluntary," she replied. "You are walking down a difficult path and everyone needs a safe place to talk from time to time. Plus, your cat has been worried about you."

That took Wilson by surprise. He didn't even know Mau

and Leader got together, much less discussed him. "She's never said anything to me," he said defensively.

Leader paused and turned her gray eyes to him. "Are you sure you just weren't listening?" She didn't wait for an answer and broke eye contact. Her window was already rolling up when she ended the encounter with a simple, "Good night, Fulcrum."

THE END

The agents of The Salt Mine will return in *High Horse*

Printed in Great Britain
by Amazon

67912357R00135